Three Truths and a Lie

Also by Brent Hartinger

The Russel Middlebrook Series

Geography Club (Book 1)

The Order of the Poison Oak (Book 2)

*Double Feature: Attack of the Soul-Sucking Brain Zombies/
Bride of the Soul-Sucking Brain Zombies* (Book 3)

The Elephant of Surprise (Book 4)

Russel Middlebrook: The Futon Years

The Thing I Didn't Know I Didn't Know (Book 1)

Barefoot in the City of Broken Dreams (Book 2)

The Road to Amazing (Book 3)

Other Books

Shadow Walkers

Project Sweet Life

Grand & Humble

The Last Chance Texaco

Three Truths and a Lie

Also by Brent Hartinger

The Russel Middlebrook Series

Geography Club (Book 1)

The Order of the Poison Oak (Book 2)

*Double Feature: Attack of the Soul-Sucking Brain Zombies/
Bride of the Soul-Sucking Brain Zombies* (Book 3)

The Elephant of Surprise (Book 4)

Russel Middlebrook: The Futon Years

The Thing I Didn't Know I Didn't Know (Book 1)

Barefoot in the City of Broken Dreams (Book 2)

The Road to Amazing (Book 3)

Other Books

Shadow Walkers

Project Sweet Life

Grand & Humble

The Last Chance Texaco

Three Truths and a Lie

BRENT HARTINGER

Simon Pulse

New York   London   Toronto   Sydney   New Delhi

SIMON PULSE

An imprint of Simon & Schuster Children's Publishing Division

1230 Avenue of the Americas, New York, New York 10020

First Simon Pulse hardcover edition August 2016

Text copyright © 2016 by Brent Hartinger

Jacket illustration by Steve Scott

Jacket illustration copyright © 2016 by Simon & Schuster, Inc.

All rights reserved, including the right of reproduction in whole or in part in any form.

SIMON PULSE and colophon are registered trademarks of Simon & Schuster, Inc.

For information about special discounts for bulk purchases, please contact Simon & Schuster Special Sales at 1-866-506-1949 or business@simonandschuster.com.

The Simon & Schuster Speakers Bureau can bring authors to your live event. For more information or to book an event contact the Simon & Schuster Speakers Bureau at 1-866-248-3049 or visit our website at www.simonspeakers.com.

Book designed by Steve Scott

The text of this book was set in ITC Berkeley Oldstyle.

Manufactured in the United States of America

2 4 6 8 10 9 7 5 3 1

This title has been cataloged with the Library of Congress.

ISBN 978-1-4814-4960-1 (hc)

ISBN 978-1-4814-4961-8 (pbk)

ISBN 978-1-4814-4962-5 (eBook)

To Michael Jensen
And to Lori Grant and Sarah Warn
Friends forever, no lie

It was my fault, everything that happened that weekend.

It's hard for me to admit that, but it's the truth. I was the one who suggested going away in the first place. If I hadn't had that dumb idea, who knows how things would've ended? Somehow, I'm going to have to live with that for the rest of my life.

But I'm getting ahead of myself. I need to start at the beginning. That's the only way you're ever going to understand what really happened.

I guess it all began with the tattoos.

It was night, and I had gone downtown with my friends Liam, Mia, and Galen. I, Rob, was getting a tattoo! We all were, matching ones. We'd come to this tattoo parlor, the single open business in a row of darkened storefronts. They say the most important thing about a tattoo parlor is that it looks clean, and this one did, mostly. But it didn't *feel* clean. Maybe it was the fact that the building was old: the linoleum was warped, and there was a mustiness in the air along with the smell of ink and rubbing alcohol and sweat. Or maybe it was because the room was filled with a zillion tattoo designs, all brightly colored, on laminated pages tacked to the walls or bound in thick albums on the coffee table. Given the dreariness of the rest of the room, and the neighborhood outside, it was like they were overdoing it, like they had something to hide.

Liam, my boyfriend, was in the tattoo chair, which was sort of like a dentist's chair. The artist was this tall, gawky woman who didn't have any tattoos herself, at least not any visible ones, which I thought was weird. She was sitting on a stool next to Liam, hunched over like a vulture eating roadkill, putting the finishing touches on this little tattoo on the inside of his wrist. It was of a spiderweb, not half an inch long.

Mia, Galen, and I were watching it all from the waiting area, about ten feet away.

"I thought you said it wouldn't hurt," Liam said, wincing repeatedly.

2

"I lied!" Mia said, letting out an actual cackle.

She and Galen had already gotten their tattoos, and now their arms were wrapped with white bandages, like they'd both tried to kill themselves by slitting their wrists. Looking back, I don't really remember which of us chose the spiderweb design or why.

Overhead, the fluorescent lights flickered. All the while, the tattoo machine buzzed. Or maybe it was more of a high-pitched whine. Anyway, I could feel the vibration of the needle through the floor, even from ten feet away. Once Liam was done, it would be my turn, and as I watched the artist work on him, I could almost feel that needle against my skin. The pricking, the stinging, the oozing of blood.

I was scared of getting a tattoo, about forty percent sure I was going to end up catching hepatitis C, or worse. But if I'm going to be honest, I was a little excited too.

Truthfully, I wasn't the kind of person who got tattoos. People always say I'm clean-cut, even wholesome, but I know what they really mean is that I'm boring. But I don't care if people sometimes ignore me, if I'm not usually the center of attention. Besides, everyone has tattoos these days, so I don't see how that gets people to pay attention to you anyway.

Liam was the same way. If anything, he was even dorkier than I was, more cautious, even more high-strung.

But that was okay. It's part of why I liked him so much. We'd only been going out for three months, but we were already in sync. People said it was kind of eerie how alike we were, but I loved it. We watched the same movies, listened to the same music, played the same video games. On our first date, at Chipotle, we ordered separately but ended up getting exactly the same thing, right down to a black bean burrito with the same two kinds of salsa, roasted chili corn and tomatillo green chili.

Outside the tattoo parlor, a car backfired and I jumped. At least I hoped it was a car. We weren't in the best part of town.

"Looks good," Mia said, staring at Liam's tattoo as the artist dabbed it with a square of bloody gauze. I wasn't sure if she was talking to me or him, but I nodded anyway.

Mia was the real reason Liam and I were even here. If Liam and I tended to blend into the background, Mia stood out like, well, a colorful tattoo parlor in a row of darkened storefronts. She was good-looking, with a mane of long brown hair and a body like she belonged on a beer poster, but that was actually the least of it. It was more her whole attitude about the world, like life was just one big dare. She could be crude and bossy and impulsive, and she did always have to be the center of attention, which sometimes got annoying. But she could also be spontaneous and fun and funny, and was probably the least pretentious, least judgmental person I've ever met. She didn't take anything too seriously for long. For her, the most important thing was having a good time. It was all about the here and now.

For weeks I'd wondered how Liam had ended up friends with someone like her. I guess they'd met early in their freshman year, back when everyone is a loser and you pick your friends because they have a locker or a desk next to you, not because you have anything in common. But for whatever reason, they'd *stayed* friends, even after Mia started running with the wolves. Now she and Liam were almost inseparable.

Truthfully, she made me uneasy. I resented how close she was with Liam. I had a few of my own friends, but nothing like what Liam had, nothing like Mia. And I wanted to be going out with Liam, not Mia. It's not just that I didn't have a lot in common with her, it's that *Liam* didn't seem to have a lot in common with her. So why were they even friends? What did it say about Liam that I didn't know why he was drawn to someone like that? Or why she was drawn to him? It was like they shared a secret I didn't know. Liam and I seemed so in sync in so many ways, but this was the one thing I didn't understand about him. And I couldn't help but wonder if it meant I didn't understand him as well as I thought.

But I'd accepted they were sort of a package deal. And it was more than just being okay with being around her. If I wanted my relationship with Liam to work, I knew Mia had to like me too. That's why I'd agreed to get this tattoo in the first place, to come along with the others. It had been Mia's idea, and Liam and Galen had seemed excited, so I hadn't said a word. I'd gone along to get along.

It wasn't *just* that. I did sort of like that Mia pushed me to do things I wouldn't do otherwise. I'd spent my whole life inside my comfort zone, which is nice and safe and predictable, but also kind of boring.

The needle kept whining as the artist put the last touches on Liam's tattoo. Soon it would be my turn. But all of a sudden my comfort zone was back to looking pretty good. What kind of idiot wanted out of their comfort zone?

"Hey," Galen said to me. "You okay?" Mia's boyfriend was part hipster, part jock. He had a body like the figure at the top of a high school trophy—lean and solid and golden—with facial hair that was a cross between a chin strip and a goatee. But the most interesting thing about him, the quality that was both hipster *and* jock, was his cool, above-it-all attitude. If Mia was a prize fighter punching her way through life, Galen was a cloud flowing around anything that got in front of him. In the few months I'd known him, I'd never seen him get upset about anything. The worst you could say about him is that he got kind of moody in the afternoons at school, but I'd always thought that was like how the animals at zoos all look listless because they're forced to live in cages.

7

"Huh?" I said to him. What had he asked me again?

"You look like you're in pain."

I wasn't in pain yet, but I could tell from Liam's expression that he was. Which meant I was going to be in pain soon too.

"No," I said, relaxing my jaw. "I'm okay."

"Hey," Galen said. "A guy with a tattoo walks into a bar and hears a voice say, 'That is a *fantastic* tattoo. And the color really goes with your eyes!' The guy looks around and doesn't see anyone, so he says to the bartender, 'Who just said that?' And the bartender says, 'The complimentary peanuts.'"

Galen laughed, and I did too, mostly because I knew Galen was trying to cheer me up, but also because he really had sold the joke. Galen told a lot of corny jokes—lately, it was the "guy walks into a bar" kind—and somehow he made those seem cool too.

"Okay," the tattoo artist said, leaning back on her stool. "You're done."

At some point, the whining of the needle had stopped. I guess Galen really had distracted me.

I looked down at Liam's wrist. It was bandaged now, like Mia's and Galen's.

8

"You're up next," the tattoo artist said.

Was she talking to me? Of course she was. There was one other person waiting, but we had come in as a group, and Mia, Galen, and Liam all had their tattoos. I was the only one who didn't.

I stood up.

"Oh shit," Galen said, turning away from the front window, giving it the cold shoulder. It was like he'd seen someone on the street outside and now didn't want them to see him.

"What is it?" Mia asked. She scratched her bandage.

"Nothing. But we need to go." There was a weird urgency in his voice—weird for anyone, but especially for Galen.

Mia looked up, confused. "What are you talking about?"

I looked out the window behind Galen. Three figures beelined toward the tattoo parlor from the other side of the street, making the cars stop right in the middle of the road. It was dark, and one of the streetlights was out, so I couldn't make out their faces, how old they were. But I could tell they were angry just by the way they were walking, the way their heads didn't bob when they moved. I could also tell they'd spotted Galen. One of the guys had his hand in the pocket of his jacket, and I didn't even want to think about what might be in there.

"It's someone I don't wanna see," Galen said. He breezed over to the front door, still not panicking exactly, but he flicked the dead bolt with a loud snap.

The tattoo artist heard the sound and looked over. "What are you doing?" she said.

"Just for a second, okay?" he said. He opened his wallet and flashed her a fan of bills, then left it all by the cash register. "Is there a back door? Where does it lead?"

"The back alley," the woman said, now weirdly indifferent, casually wrestling with a package containing a fresh tattoo needle.

Maybe she was used to this kind of thing, but I sure wasn't.

"Come on," Galen said, commanding Mia, Liam, and me like dogs, leading us toward the exit.

I was about to point out that I still hadn't gotten my tattoo, but then I remembered I hadn't even wanted that tattoo to begin with.

We hustled to the back door. Behind us, someone

yanked on the locked front door, and the windows rattled.

Galen threw open the rear door and the four of us stepped out into the night. There was hardly any light in the alley. After all the bright colors in the tattoo parlor, it felt like stepping into a black-and-white movie, like stepping from Oz back into Kansas.

Galen turned left and slipped off into the darkness. I could hear the thump of his footsteps—he was already running. I wanted to ask him what was going on, call out for an explanation, but none of us dared make a sound. Instead, Mia, Liam, and I hurried after him, past Dumpsters and garbage cans. A TV blared out of one of the windows above us, music from some soapy romance.

"Galen!" someone called from behind us, a voice that cracked like a whip. "I know it's you, you asshole! You better *hope* we don't catch you!"

At the end of the darkened alley, the streetlights shone down like the glow from the top of an aquarium. But right in front of me, Galen's silhouette turned sharply right, disappearing into a slash of darkness.

"In here!" he said. "Quickly!"

It was some sort of side alley, really narrow, sandwiched between two buildings. Too narrow for Dumpsters or even garbage cans.

A figure stepped into the aquarium glow at the end of the main alley—someone different from the person behind us. Whoever was chasing us must have split up and circled around to cover both ends of the alley. The person in front of us had his hand in the pocket of his jacket again.

I followed Galen into the side alley. It was even darker than the main alley, like a black curtain had fallen behind me. There may not have been any cans, but there was plenty of garbage. I scrambled over it in the dark, sometimes tripping, sometimes slipping in slick, gooey pools. This was exactly the kind of place where you'd step on a nail, but that was the least of my worries now. My pulse pounded and I sucked down the foul, oily air. I was desperate to get to the end of the alley. Did Galen know where he was going? What if there was someone waiting for us there too? What the hell was that nonsense about my wanting to leave my comfort zone?

12

A wooden fence blocked our way, the dead end of a maze.

My pulse pounded, and now I couldn't even breathe.

"Climb!" Galen said, already clawing his way up. "Just *climb*!"

I searched for the cross-slats in the dark—something to hold on to. The wood was old and splitting, and I could already tell I was going to get splinters, but I climbed anyway. The four of us fumbled our way upward, and the boards squeaked around me like rats. The fence was narrow, the width of the alley, so we jostled against one another, a little like rats ourselves. Someone even kicked me in the head, but I couldn't make out who it was in the dark.

Finally, my hands reached the top and I pulled myself up into the light. The others had beaten me over the fence and were now standing on the other side.

"Hurry!" Mia said.

I lowered myself down.

After the darkness of the alley, the streetlights and colors on the other side of the fence were blinding—we'd stepped back into Oz. We were on a different street on a different block, but it wouldn't take a genius to figure out where we'd gone.

A taxi glided down the street in front of us.

Galen leaped out into the street in front of the cab. "Stop!" he said. "Stop!"

The tires squealed, but at least it stopped. The taxi's light was on, which I guess meant it was vacant.

We climbed into the cab—I took the front seat—and slammed the doors. A figure appeared at the far end of the street, hand in pocket. I still couldn't see his face, but I knew his eyes were tracking us.

"Go!" Galen said to the driver.

The driver sped off, and I gripped the armrests. I had splinters from the fence, just like I'd thought.

As we passed the corner, I ducked down. If that guy really did have a gun in his pocket, who's to say he wouldn't use it?

"What about my car?" Mia said.

"We'll come back *later*," Galen said, a whispered hiss, even more urgent than before.

That shut Mia up. After that, we all held our breath—even the driver, I think.

14

Finally, a couple of blocks later, Mia sat upright again. "Okay, what the fuck, Galen?"

Galen shrugged innocently, and somehow, even after everything that had happened, he sold that too. "That wasn't anyone. A guy and his friends. He's a dick."

Mia just glared at him.

"Okay, I may have screwed his girlfriend. Twice. But this was *way* before I met you."

Mia rolled her eyes, and I glanced over at the cab driver. His face was flat and his eyes were fixed straight ahead. I guess when you drive a taxi, you're supposed to pretend you can't hear what your passengers are saying, like they're not really there.

"Well, that was two firsts in one night," Liam said. "My first tattoo and my first time almost roughed up by thugs." He hesitated a perfect second, then cracked a smile. "I can't think of the last time I had so much fun!"

Mia and Galen laughed.

That's when I finally knew why Liam was friends with Mia. It was so obvious. He craved the excitement, just like I did.

Except I *hadn't* craved the excitement. At the first sign of danger, I'd wanted to scamper right back into my comfort zone. I'd been worried about splinters and getting shot. So did that mean Liam and I weren't as in sync as I'd thought?

I looked at the three of them squeezed together in the back-seat. Liam stared out his window, and Mia, sitting in the middle, leaned over to kiss Galen. Even in the dark, I could see the white bandages on their wrists, which they weren't supposed to take off for at least ten hours. Liam, Galen, and Mia all had matching tattoos under those bandages, but I didn't. I had nothing. That made me feel even more left out. But we couldn't go back to the tattoo parlor now, not with Galen's enemies around.

"Where to?" the driver asked us, and Mia told him.

But that got me thinking.

"We should go away," I said to the others. "For the week-end. Somewhere private. Somewhere where it'd be just us."

"I wish," Mia said. "Where would we go?"

"How about your parents' cabin?" Galen said. He was back to being completely cool again, no sign of stress at all. "Out on the Olympic Peninsula."

The Olympic Peninsula is what people call the northwest corner of Washington State. It's across Puget Sound from Seattle, and the only way to get there is to take a ferry, or drive around way down south and up again. So it's actually pretty remote. It's mostly mountains and forests and rivers, and there isn't a single big city.

"I haven't been up there in forever," Mia said. She looked over at Galen, frowning. "How do you even know about that?"

"I saw a photo at your house, and I asked your parents about it."

"I doubt my parents'll let me go," Liam said. "Not that far. Not for two nights."

This was going to be a problem. Galen's mom was almost completely absent and his dad had left town years ago, but Liam's parents were really overprotective. Frankly, I wondered how he was going to explain the tattoo.

"So lie and tell them you're staying at my house," Mia said to Liam. "You've spent the night there before, lots of times. And if they do find out we left, we can say it was, like, a last-minute thing."

Liam thought about it. Mia's parents were strict too, which is part of the reason why Liam's parents let him spend the night at her house. Plus, everyone knew he was gay.

As for my parents, I knew they might object at first, but they'd let me go in the end. My parents could be annoyingly reasonable. All my life, they'd seemed to know exactly when to give me the right amount of freedom. I was eighteen now, graduating from high school in a few weeks, and I knew they'd see this as the perfect chance for me to test my independence before going off to college in the fall. Unlike everyone else in that car, if I ever screwed up my life, I wouldn't be able to blame absent or overprotective parents. I wouldn't be able to blame anyone except myself.

"I'm in," Galen said.

"Okay," Liam said. "Let's do it."

I smiled.

It's hard for me to talk about that conversation in the taxi. If I'd never suggested going away, I wouldn't have reminded Galen about Mia's parents' cabin. We never would've gone away. None of what happened that weekend would've happened.

That's what I mean about this being all my fault.

It's hard for me to talk about that conversation in the taxi. But that's easy compared to talking about everything that came next.

There was something off about Marot, Washington.

Marot is this nothing little town in the middle of the Olympic Peninsula that we had to pass through on the way to Mia's parents' cabin. It was a big timber hub for a long time, but by the 1980s, they had cut down most of the peninsula's old growth forests, which is where the real money is, and started using new machines that eliminated most of the jobs. So times had been a lot tougher since then.

But you already know this, don't you? Of course you do. Anyway, maybe that's why the town felt the way it did—like a ghost who doesn't realize he's already dead.

We'd left for the cabin from school Friday afternoon, right after lunch. Mia and Galen had wanted to skip completely, but even if it was only two weeks until graduation, Liam and I were worried about how it would look. I was seventy percent sure it wasn't true what they say, that once you've been accepted into a college, they don't care what your last transcript looks like, so we compromised and just skipped the last two classes.

By the time we reached Marot, we'd been driving for over three hours straight, and we were all ready for a break. Mia parked the car along the street—the entire downtown was only about a block and a half long—and we all climbed out. The air smelled like pine and rotting garbage, and the sky was overcast, a dirty air filter needing to be replaced.

It felt a little like we'd gone back in time. Except for a couple of gas stations on the outskirts of town, there probably hadn't been any new buildings built in Marot since the 1950s. The signs on the stores all used old-fashioned fonts. The word DRUGS! was painted on the side of the pharmacy in big happy letters, like drugs were something to be really excited about, not something kids should be terrified of.

But it didn't really seem like the 1950s either. For one thing, everything was faded and dirty and run-down. At least half the stores were boarded up, and there were too many power lines overhead, a couple that were drooping badly. Despite what the sign said, somehow I doubted that the pie in the diner really was world-famous.

The people didn't look particularly cheerful and friendly either, at least not the ones we saw shuffling along the sidewalks and milling in the grocery store parking lot. The men all seemed to have wild beards and pot bellies, and the women had greasy hair and bad skin. Everyone was wearing thick boots and flannel and denim.

And everyone was old. The only people we saw under the age of forty were a couple of skinny guys our age leaning against their cars, slouching like a pair of parentheses. They weren't on smartphones or anything.

Their eyes flicked our way, and I nodded awkwardly, but they didn't respond.

"I need to pee," Mia said. She started for a nearby store—sporting goods, not so surprising in a town surrounded by wilderness.

We started down the sidewalk. This woman was coming toward us, approaching like a bulldozer. She was older, in her sixties maybe, with short white hair and a face like turkey jerky, sort of a leathery pinkish brown.

And she had a crossbow strapped to her back. No, seriously, with a quiver and everything. But even a crossbow didn't seem all that strange in a place like Marot. That was the other thing I noticed about this town: people definitely liked their weapons. There were rifles in the window of the sporting goods store, and a full gun rack in the back of the pickup truck parked next to us. One of the skinny guys leaning against those cars had even started whittling with a switchblade.

"Mrs. Brummit?" Mia said.

Mia *knew* the woman with the turkey jerky face? Then again, we were going to her family's cabin, not too far away, so it made sense that she might know some of the people in Marot.

The woman's pale blue eyes focused, the wheels in her head starting to turn.

"You probably don't remember me," Mia went on. "I'm Mia Kinnaman. From my parents' cabin up at the lake? My friends and I were just heading up there now. It's sure a coincidence, running into you like this."

"I know who you are," Mrs. Brummit said, in a voice that could have frozen warts off fingers.

She remembered Mia all right, and she sure wasn't happy about it.

There was an awkward silence. Maybe all the people in Marot were this rude. It did suddenly seem like the whole town was staring at us—not just the skinny guys leaning against their cars and the woman with the turkey jerky face. I finally noticed an actual kid, a pale girl on her bicycle, but she was scowling at us too.

It took more than this to intimidate Mia. She looked at Mrs. Brummit and said, "Well, okay then." And then she stepped to one side and headed down the sidewalk. Galen, Liam, and I scampered after her like little ducklings after their mother.

Once we were out of earshot, Liam said, "What was that about?"

"Oh, who the fuck knows?" she said, shrugging off the whole interaction. "She and her family own the cabin near ours, but I guess she's mad about something. Maybe I borrowed their raft without asking back when I was nine years old."

I glanced back at Mrs. Brummit, half expecting her to have disappeared, like she'd never been there at all. But no, she was still there, glaring back at me like my own reflection in a mirror.

The sporting goods store was much larger inside than it had looked from the outside. It was definitely bigger than the pharmacy, and maybe even bigger than the grocery story.

It was full of weapons, mostly guns and knives. It was kind of crazy, this giant open space crammed full of things that shoot and cut, all stuff that's designed to kill. There were also fishing poles and nets and, yeah, bows and arrows, and there must have been nonlethal stuff too—I remember a brand of camouflage clothing, RobGear, because it was my first name. But what struck me most were the guns and knives. Barrels and blades. The store smelled like leather and glue and something stinky, like someone had recently opened the refrigerator with the fish bait in it.

On the way to the restroom, Mia stopped at a rack of T-shirts. I sidled up next to her.

"Do you really think it was just that you borrowed their raft without asking?" I asked.

"What?" she said. This was classic Mia. She'd already put what had happened out on the sidewalk behind her. But I wasn't like that. Our encounter with Mrs. Brummit had shaken me.

"The woman," I said.

"Hey, what do you think?" She held a shirt up to her chest that read, SPOTTED OWL TASTES LIKE CHICKEN.

The spotted owl is an endangered species that keeps loggers from cutting down certain trees and forests.

"Nice," I said, but it felt a little like she was blowing me off. And it still felt weird being surrounded by all those weapons. Right in front of me was a case full of giant knives and cleavers, probably for butchering deer.

An aisle away, Galen stood facing a shelf full of a dozen different kinds of bug spray. I drifted over to him and said, "There's something not right about this town."

Galen looked over at me, his face almost completely blank. "Huh?"

I remembered it was the middle of the afternoon and he was never very sharp this time of day.

"Forget it," I said. Finally, I walked over to Liam, who was staring up at an elk head mounted on the wall. That was the other thing this store had lots of—stuffed elk and deer and moose heads. There was even a whole big stuffed black bear in the middle of the store, standing upright with its teeth bared and its arms and claws stretched out.

Liam turned to me, his eyes wide, and said, "Rob, didn't you think that was weird, that woman out on the sidewalk?" He shook his head. "There's something off about this town."

I wanted to give him a big hug, but I figured that might not go over well in a place like this, so I smiled and said, "*Totally* off."

At least Liam knew how I felt.

Ten minutes later, Mia found Liam and me in the back of the store.

"Have you seen Galen?" she said.

"What?" I said. "No. Why?"

"He's gone. And he isn't answering my texts."

Clutching her phone, she glanced around, almost twitching. She looked different than I'd ever seen her before—face drawn, eyebrows furrowed.

Mia was scared.

She hadn't looked like this out on the sidewalk when she'd been confronted by Mrs. Brummit, and I'm not even sure she'd looked like this that night at the tattoo parlor. Seeing Mia worried, that rattled me more than anything that had happened so far.

We glanced around the store for Galen. There were lots of different racks and display cases, plus the refrigerator and the stuffed bear. He could have been behind any of them.

"He has to be here somewhere," I said.

"Maybe the bathroom?" Liam said.

Mia shook her head. "I was just there."

Up at the front of the store, a bell rang—that familiar double ring of the door to a store opening or closing. We couldn't see it, but someone was entering or leaving.

"Maybe he left," I said.

"Why would he leave?" Mia said, worried again.

Mia sent him another text, and I started poking around the store looking for him. There weren't *that* many places he could be.

As I searched, I suddenly had the feeling I was being watched. It absolutely felt like there were eyes on me, following me.

Then I realized it was just the mounted animal heads on the walls, and I immediately felt stupid.

Even so, I couldn't help but wonder exactly how off this town was. How mad was Mrs. Brummit at Mia for stealing that raft? Could someone have done something to Galen? Could we all be in some sort of danger? It was hard to ignore the guns and knives all around me, the barrels and blades. There was a rack of gunsights pointed right at me, one that even said it had night vision.

I sensed someone staring at me again, peering in through the front window from the sidewalk. Did they have short white hair and a pink turkey jerky face? But when I looked, there wasn't anyone there.

I really needed to get a grip.

"Mia?" I said.

"What?" she said, not far away.

At that exact moment, Galen stepped out from behind the bear in the middle of the store. He saw us looking at him and lifted his arms like the bear and let out a big roar.

Then he laughed.

He breezed closer to us, a stupid grin on his face.

"So a bear walks into a bar," Galen said, "and he says to the bartender, 'I want a beer and'"—he stopped for a long moment—"'an order of nachos.' And the bartender says, 'Hey, what's with the big paws?'"

Needless to say, Galen's bout of afternoon moodiness was over. And the concern was already gone from Mia's face.

When we got back to our car, I half expected Mrs. Brummit to have poked holes in our tires with the arrows from her crossbow, or maybe to have scraped the word "Beware!" in the paint on the door. But it was all fine. People weren't staring at us anymore either. Everything was normal. Yes, Mrs. Brummit had given Mia a dirty look. So what? Everything else that had happened in town—the staring, the would-be face in the window, even the feeling that something was off—

I was ninety percent sure it had all been in my mind.

We missed the cutoff to Mia's parents' cabin.

Even Mia, who had been up there lots of times, didn't see it. Maybe she'd been more shaken up by what had happened in town than she let on. But it didn't take her long to realize we'd gone too far and we had to backtrack.

The cutoff was right off the main highway, and it was pretty easy to miss. It was nothing more than a dirt logging road that immediately disappeared into a dense evergreen forest.

A rain forest.

That part of the Olympic Peninsula is mostly rain forest. When most people hear "rain forest," they think of a tropical jungle. But these are temperate rain forests, which mean they get just as much rain as a tropical rain forest—even more, in some cases—but they grow in colder climates. Places like the coast of Washington State.

But you probably already know all this too, right?

Anyway, the trees were thick and wet and droopy, and covered with hanging moss, so the cutoff into the forest was dark. It looked more like the entrance to a cave.

Mia drove inside. Twenty feet later, we came to a metal gate. I could see the thick padlock from the car.

"It's okay," Mia said, fumbling in a bag on the floor. "I've got a key." Once she found it, she climbed out of the car to open the gate.

Water dripped down all around us, jostling the ferns, even though it hadn't been raining. I hadn't been in the rain forest too many times before, but I guess the water is almost always dripping down from the trees and the hanging moss. The sound is hard to describe. It doesn't sound like rain. It's not as even or consistent. It's slower, lazier. You never know when or where the next drop's going to fall.

It felt like we'd gone back in time again, but not to the

1950s. Now we'd gone back a million years, before the existence of humans.

"Lock it after us," I said to Mia, meaning the gate, after she returned to the car. I was still mostly sure the strange things that had happened in town had all been in my mind, but there was that ten percent of me that thought maybe they weren't.

Beyond the gate, we started making our way along the road. I stared out the window of the car, finally starting to get used to the gloom of the ancient rain forest and the water dripping on the windows.

All of a sudden, the trees disappeared.

We'd followed the road right out into a clear-cut. This made sense—it was a logging road, after all. Do any hiking in western Washington and you quickly learn the game of deception that the logging companies all play: they leave the trees intact right along the highways to make people think there's a lot more forest than there is. That way they can fool people into thinking Washington, the Evergreen State, really is still evergreen. At least for the people who never get out of their cars. It's only once you get a few hundred feet beyond the main roads that you realize it's all a big lie and that the state's "forests" are mostly a depressing patchwork of clear-cuts and tree farms.

I should have expected it, but I didn't. The loggers had mowed the entire forest down, leaving nothing but a stretch of stumps, some piles of dead, ragged branches, and a lot of deep tire tracks. The rain forest had been dark and misty, but this was the exact opposite. The clouds had broken and the late afternoon sun was suddenly shining all around us. But it was in a place where the sun *shouldn't* have been shining. Where maybe it hadn't shone for thousands or possibly even millions of years.

In the front seat, Mia and Galen chattered away, but the clear-cut depressed me. This was all the same land, but the forested and deforested parts didn't just look different; they *felt* different. One felt right, and the other felt very, very wrong.

Opposite me, Liam stared listlessly out his own window.

Before long, we entered the dark, misty rain forest again. This time it felt like burrowing under a blanket—comforting. But I knew I shouldn't get too cozy.

Sure enough, a few minutes later, we drove into another dazzling clear-cut. It was a little bewildering, alternating between forest and clear-cuts like that, like being in a room with a kid flicking on and off the light switch.

The bottom of our car scraped the road. The logging trucks that had traveled here before us were so heavy that they'd created deep grooves with their big tires. That left a rocky bulge in the middle of the road, and we could hear the gravel clacking and scraping against the metal of the car whenever the tracks got too deep.

Each time it happened, Galen would say, "Slow down." But it didn't seem like Mia ever did.

The road kept alternating between forest and clear-cut, so much so that I was getting dizzy. Meanwhile, the road also started splitting into branches. The network of back-country logging roads was like a maze, and none of the roads were marked. If you didn't know which way to go, you'd be lost in a matter of minutes. Mia's parents had insisted she take a map, but Mia had spaced and left it behind. Still, she always seemed to know exactly which road to take. She'd been up here dozens of times with her family, even if it had been years ago. I told myself that was enough, that we were fine relying on Mia's memory. Then again, she had missed the original turnoff.

We drove on like that for more than an hour, passing through clear-cuts and rain forest, Mia picking the turns. How far was it really? It was hard to say, since we never hit more than ten miles an hour on the twisty road.

Finally, we started down a steep hill, then turned a corner and came upon a body of water that was bigger than a pond but not quite a lake. It was roughly circular, maybe a quarter mile across. Around a little less than half the lake, the rain forest grew right up to the water, and usually *over* the water, with the trees and ferns reaching out like the crowds at some presidential rally, trying to touch the candidate.

But the forest on the other half of the lake had been clear-cut. There was a little buffer of trees around the shore itself, but the land beyond that had been mowed completely bare. Plus, that part of the forest had been a hillside, so the clear-cut dominated the lake more than the forest on the other half did.

We all climbed out of the car and faced the devastation.

"Nice," Liam said.

"Oh yeah," Mia said. "That's why my family stopped coming up here. I just remembered."

"Because of the clear-cut?" I asked.

She nodded. "My grandparents owned that land. They'd planned to give it to my dad as an inheritance, but they had some investments go bad or something, and they had to sell. They only kept the land right around their cabin. The logging company said they wouldn't ever clear-cut, but then they went ahead and did it anyway." She thought for a second, then said, "Fuck, that's probably why Mrs. Brummit was such a bitch back in town. It sort of ruined the lake. I think they ended up having money problems too, but with that clear-cut, no one wanted to buy their place. They were really pissed off."

"Where do the Brummits live?" Galen asked.

"At the end of the road." Mia nodded toward the dirt road we'd come in on. I hadn't even noticed that it kept going, that it disappeared into the rain forest again. "But they don't *live* there. It's a vacation cabin, like ours."

The view was depressing, and the ground was wet, even in the area around the cabin where there weren't any trees. The road itself was downright muddy, and everything else was this sort of grassy moss, maybe like peat moss. It was like walking on a sponge. It made the whole world unsteady, and it took me a minute to figure out my balance.

The cabin itself was a squat, lumpy thing about a hundred feet up from the lake. The roof looked like it was made entirely of moss. The whole thing was smaller than I expected, one room or maybe two. It had been built from some dark, ancient wood, probably from the surrounding forests, but it didn't look sturdy. Sandwiched between all that moss, it was like the whole cabin was sinking, like the forest was slowly reclaiming its wood.

Beyond the cabin, farther from the lake, was an outhouse— Mia had already told us there was no running water. Between the cabin and the outhouse, there was a large metal barrel. Maybe it had once been used for collecting rainwater, but it was too rusted now. In front of the cabin, between it and the lake, there was an old-fashioned water pump rising out of the ground, with a small porcelain basin underneath the spout.

We all walked closer to the cabin.

It was so quiet. It was like the only sounds in the whole forest were the dripping of water from the trees around us, and now our shoes squishing in the mud and moss.

The air smelled wet. It felt wet too. It's actually hard to explain. It was confusing too, because water is supposed to be wet and air is supposed to be dry. Suddenly everything was all mixed up.

A droplet hit the surface of the water in the porcelain basin under the pump, making a *plunk* and a small ripple. It was a good twenty feet from the closest tree, so I wondered where the drop had come from, what had made the ripple. Condensation on the pump?

"Does the lake have a name?" Liam asked.

"Moon Lake," Mia said.

"Hey, the door's unlocked," Galen said.

I turned. He'd already pushed the door open.

"This far out, if someone really wants in, they're just going to break in anyway," Mia said. "Why not leave the door unlocked and save yourself a broken window or a kicked-in door? That's what my dad says anyway."

Mia and I followed Galen into the cabin.

It was what a real estate agent might call rustic or cozy, but it was mostly just a dump. Completely bare bones. Mia's grandparents had probably built the thing themselves on weekends. And then came sixty years of decay. Now it smelled musty, like rotting wood—like a wet crawl space, not a dusty attic.

There was a small kitchen area to the left of the door with some basic cupboards, a cooking area, a sink with a drain but no running water, and a cast iron wood-burning stove.

Directly in front of us, in the main room, there was a ratty old sofa and chairs in front of a brick fireplace. Beyond that was a door to what must have been a single bedroom. To my right a ladder stretched up to what looked like a sleeping loft. Directly under the loft was the dining area with a small table and chairs.

I figured Mia and Galen would get the bedroom, but at least Liam and I would have a little bit of privacy this weekend, up in the loft.

Since the cabin had no electricity, there were no lights, just kerosene lamps and candles scattered around the room. There was no refrigerator either, but we'd brought a cooler.

I took a step forward and something crunched under my feet.

"Shit," Mia said.

"What?" Liam said.

"No, really. Shit. On the floor. Animal shit. The mice and rats get inside, especially in the winter. My dad's tried everything to keep them out, but nothing works."

Sure enough, the floor was covered with these little black pellets. I hadn't noticed them against the old dark wood of the floor. Now that I looked, I saw they were everywhere, even on the kitchen countertops.

"Um, *disgusting*," Liam said.

"At least there were no raccoons or skunks," Mia said. "You don't wanna see what kinda mess they make."

As I looked closer, I noticed something else in the cabin. There were spiderwebs, all over the place. Real ones, not like the fake ones you see in the movies.

In other words, our lodging was a complete dump. I was forty percent sure I was going to catch hantavirus from the mouse droppings. Plus, we had to stare at that ugly clear-cut all weekend long.

41

So far, things weren't turning out like they were supposed to at all.

But Mia didn't hesitate. She broke out a broom and mop and ammonia, and sent Galen to pound out the mattresses and the furniture cushions. Liam and I used rags to take care of the spiderwebs. They were surprisingly strong, so thick they made a little ripping noise when you tore them away. At least we didn't see any spiders—I guess it was the wrong time of year.

The webs reminded me of the matching tattoos the others got. Their bandages were off now, revealing the little black design slowly healing on their wrists. I had a feeling we'd never go back to that tattoo parlor. I could go back on my own, get the tattoo myself, but I knew that wouldn't be the same.

"This isn't so bad," Mia said, sweeping the floor.

This was one of the things I liked about Mia: she could be a brat, but not about things she didn't have any control over, things like this.

For the next thirty minutes, we cleaned the cabin, sweeping and mopping and wiping up spiderwebs. Whenever I thought I had them all, I'd see another one.

But eventually we were done, and the cabin was clean.

Then we unloaded our bags and groceries. At least the mice hadn't gotten into the cupboards.

By the time we were finished unpacking, the floor still wasn't dry. I guess things take forever to dry in a rain forest. Or maybe they never dry out completely.

Mia took what looked like a walkie-talkie out of one of her bags and put it on the counter. "What's that?" Galen asked.

"A satellite phone," she said. "My parents made me bring it. There's no cell phone reception out here, so they wanted us to have some way to call into town in case of an emergency." She looked around in a couple of the bags. "Fuck, I forgot the marshmallows. We were coming to a cabin by a lake, how could I forget the marshmallows?" She seemed more upset about this than she had been about forgetting the map.

"Forget the marshmallows," I said. "Forget the mouse poop. We're here, we're completely on our own, and we're going to have a great weekend." For once, I was determined to be the one looking on the bright side, to be living in the here and now.

"Damn straight," Galen said. "Now let's go skinny-dipping!"

Five minutes later, we were all down at the lake, standing on the moss above this little tiny beach of grainy sand, staring out at the water.

I couldn't believe we were actually doing this. Skinny-dipping? With Galen and Mia? What if I got, uh, excited? I don't know if I mentioned this before, but Galen was a pretty good-looking guy. The last thing in the world I wanted was to see him naked. I didn't want to see anyone except Liam naked, at least not when I was naked too. I'd always been able to control myself in the locker room at school, but I'd had a few close calls, barely making it into my underwear in time.

And then there was Mia seeing *me* naked. I didn't want her laughing at me, or comparing me to Liam. He and I were actually both about the same size, not massive, but nothing to be embarrassed about either. On the other hand, it was cold outside, and the water was probably cold too.

But it's not like I could say no to skinny-dipping, not without looking like a complete idiot.

None of us had started undressing yet, and I think it had something to do with the light. It was twilight, the exact moment between day and night. It was sort of breathtaking. With everything so dark, you couldn't make out the devastation on the other side of the lake, but you could still see the lake itself. The water lapped gently against the shore, and the fish were feeding, so everywhere you looked there was a splash, like giant raindrops. I imagined I'd somehow become miniaturized, and I was standing at the edge of a puddle at the start of a rainstorm. The universe was suddenly such a massive, awesome place, and I knew deep in my bones that I was just this tiny, completely insignificant part of it, but somehow that made it all even more amazing.

"Well?" Galen said, breaking the silence.

"This was *your* idea," Mia said. "That means *you* go first."

"You guys are such pussies!" Galen said, suddenly kicking off his shoes, then shucking off his shirt.

"Are we sure we want to do this?" Liam said. "It's going to be cold."

"*Really* cold," Mia said. "I doubt there's been a single really sunny day since winter."

"I mean it," Galen said. "Pussies!" At that, he yanked down his pants, boxers and all, and kicked them aside.

I was standing behind him, and I made a point not to stare. But he had the kind of ass that was impossible not to notice—round and dimpled. His back was incredible too, lean and rippled with muscles. Then there were his shoulders and arms, which were the best kind of broad, like those of a natural athlete, not the kind of a guy who is a slave to the gym and his protein supplements. His whole body was this golden brown, like the toasted marshmallows we weren't going to be having that weekend. How was it that he didn't have tan lines? And if there was hair on his legs, it was lighter than the stuff on his head, so his whole body looked hairless, like he'd been buffed clean. Then again, I was only seeing him from behind.

And like I said, I wasn't staring.

I glanced over at Liam. He was not staring about as well as I was.

Galen entered the water like a skydiver leaping from a plane.

When he resurfaced a good fifteen feet from shore, he turned back around toward us, treading water. The lake was black and the light was low, so anything below his chest had disappeared down into the murk.

"It's not that cold," he said.

"Really?" I asked optimistically.

"No," Mia said. "He's so lying." But she was already undressing.

I'm as gay as they come, but even I could see that she was just as stunning as Galen. For some reason, I didn't expect the two of them to have such good posture. They were like the underwear models in an advertising supplement, proud and confident.

She made her own flying leap into the water, exactly like I knew she would.

And when she surfaced, she said, "Fuck, fuck, fuck!"

The water gurgled near the beach. While I'd been busy making sure not to stare at Galen, Liam had undressed and was slowly easing his way into the lake too. He was already in up to his waist, arms raised.

"Come on," Galen said. "Just get it over with all at once."

"Yeah, just go for it," Mia said.

But Liam ignored them, slowly sliding the rest of the way in. "Jesus," he said, "that's cold!" I noticed he'd kept his glasses on.

"Hey, I bet I know why this is called Moon Lake," Galen said.

He did a surface dive, mooning us all with his golden ass.

Mia laughed, and Liam gasped again, but I wasn't sure if it was from the cold or Galen's perfect ass.

Standing on the shore of that lake, I felt small again, but not because it was twilight and everything felt breathtaking. It was because I was self-conscious. Everyone else was in the lake now, and I was alone, still dressed, up on land.

I slipped off my shirt and wrestled with the button on my jeans.

Down in the water, Galen howled like a wolf, and Mia laughed again.

"No, seriously," Galen said. "Maybe it's werewolves. Wasn't that stupid vampire movie set somewhere around here?"

I stepped out of my socks and pants and drifted closer to the lake, tentative, cupping myself. When I stepped into the water, it was so cold that I didn't feel anything at all, just this dull anesthetizing ache. Then the lake sloshed up against my ankles, and I gasped too.

In the lake, Galen howled again, and Mia splashed him.

This was ironic. I'd been so worried about people seeing me naked, but now no one was even noticing me. I'd been self-conscious for nothing.

I slid into the water, halfway between Galen's wild jump and Liam's slow ease. I braced myself for the sting of the cold, but it never quite came.

"It's really not that bad," Galen said, meaning the water. "I told you guys."

He was actually right. Now that I was all the way in, there was something about the stillness of the water at twilight that made it seem warmer than it was. There was also something about the skinny-dipping itself. The water was touching me in places I'd never been touched by anyone except Liam. It was weirdly liberating.

But Liam said, "You're crazy!" And his teeth chattered.

Galen laughed. "Just keep moving. You'll warm up." Then he leaned back in the water, floating, and anything I hadn't seen from behind, I was seeing it now—a tangle of brown hair and other body parts bobbing up from out of the darkness. Was Galen flirting with us? Had he noticed Liam and me sneaking a peek and now was giving us a show? It's not like he'd be the first straight guy who got off on the attention of gay guys.

Liam paddled away.

"My brother used to tell me there was a Moon Lake monster," Mia said. "I was always so fucking scared."

"I'll give you a Moon Lake monster," Galen said, but rather than dunk her like I expected, his arms encircled her, pulling her close.

"How deep is the lake?" Liam asked.

Mia pushed away from Galen. "Deep enough that if you drop a reel, your dad gets really, really pissed at you." She treaded water. "It's not as cold as I thought it'd be, but it's still too damn cold. I'm getting out."

She swam for shore.

I looked at Liam. I could tell he wanted to get out too.

"Pussy!" Galen said to Mia.

"You call me that one more time," she said, stepping up onto the beach, "and you can be damn sure you won't be getting any this weekend. I mean, if you think a pussy is such a bad thing. . . ."

Liam snorted.

"I take it back!" Galen shouted.

As Mia dried herself with a towel, Galen followed her up out of the lake like Poseidon emerging from the sea. Their bodies were both so annoying with their toned calves and impossibly flat stomachs. Against that backdrop of ferns, they looked like Adam and Eve.

Galen shook his head like some kind of longhaired dog—"Hey!" Mia said—and naturally his hair ended up perfectly tousled. Unlike Mia, he didn't turn away to dry himself off. No, he turned around to face Liam and me, both of us still in the lake. Then, legs spread wide, he briskly toweled his back, making absolutely no effort to cover himself. Down below his waist, he flopped and jiggled. It was kind of impossible not to feel a little inadequate, given that's what he looked like even after a cold swim. I'd been worried about Mia comparing me to Liam.

Galen kept drying off, and he had to know Liam and I were staring. I even thought I saw him smirking. Now I knew for a fact that he was one of those straight guys who got off being ogled by gay guys.

Between Galen drying off in front of us and the lake touching me in places only Liam had ever touched me before, it was all too much. I climbed out of the water, half cupping myself again. It was definitely like those times in the locker room when I'd just barely made it into my underwear in time. But I reached my towel before anything was too obvious, and then I made a point to keep myself strategically covered.

As Galen dried himself, I spotted something on his skin. At first I thought it might be another tattoo, but no, he actually had a flaw after all—a dark mark in his armpit. It was some kind of port-wine stain, or maybe it was just a rash.

"Liam," Mia called, "you coming?"

We all turned around to look at him, treading water in the lake. Mia was already fully dressed, and I was wrapped in a towel, but Galen was still completely starkers.

"It's okay," Liam said. "I'll be there in a minute."

This was strange. He'd wanted to go skinny-dipping even less than me. And he'd also complained about the cold.

Galen faced the lake, still completely naked, the towel at his side. "Oh, Liam," he said in this really serious voice, "don't tell me we have an engorgement situation."

I looked back to Liam. Even in the dark, I somehow knew he was blushing. All Galen's strutting and preening had had an effect on Liam. It was like me, except Liam hadn't made it to his towel in time.

"Even in the cold water?" Galen said, wiggling his hips. "Damn, I'm *flattered*."

Liam turned away again.

"Galen," Mia said. "Knock it off."

I didn't know what to say. Galen was joking. Wasn't he?

Somehow it felt like a step beyond that, like some weird, complicated kind of bullying. Can a straight guy bully a gay guy by showing him his dick?

Mia led Galen away from the lake, even as Galen kept laughing, and by the time Liam climbed up out of the water, he was shaking. I couldn't help but notice he was also still fully hard.

"You okay?" I asked as he started to towel off. Liam and Galen had never really gotten along. I guess they somehow threatened each other—Mia's boyfriend and her best friend in conflict.

"I'm *fine*," Liam said.

But he wasn't fine. And I really couldn't blame him.

The lake may have been warmer than I expected, but we felt the cold later, when we were back in the cabin. It took forever to light a fire, even with fresh wood, a stack of newspapers, and a big box of blue-tipped matches. The fireplace hadn't been used in three years, so the chimney was full of birds' nests and more spiderwebs that I hadn't thought to clear. And even after it was lit, we all sat there shaking until the heat finally—*finally*—began to seep into the cabin.

"Man, I'm starving," Galen said. "I'd kill for a pizza right about now."

"We could order one," Mia said, wrapped in an afghan on the sofa.

"Really?" I said. "How?"

Mia gestured over to the countertop. "The satellite phone. Things are different out on the Peninsula. Businesses have to be flexible. Half the people out here live in cabins in the forest."

"It took us an hour to drive in here," Liam pointed out.

"Yeah," Mia admitted. "We'd have to meet the pizza guy, especially since we locked the gate. It probably isn't worth it."

I glanced over to where Mia had gestured at the counter where she'd put the phone earlier.

"Where's the satellite phone?" I said.

I was certain it had been there before. But it wasn't there now.

After a couple of seconds, Mia said, "What the fuck? Who moved the phone?"

We all kept staring over at the counter where the phone had been.

"I didn't," Galen said.

"I didn't either," Liam said as I nodded no too.

Still wrapped in the blanket, Mia got up and walked over to the counter. "I remember I put it right here." She turned to Galen. "Didn't I?"

"Yeah," he said. "I guess so."

"So someone must've moved it." She poked around the kitchen, looking into cupboards and drawers. "Who was it?"

I couldn't help but think of Mrs. Brummit and how she'd acted back in town. Now we knew why she was so upset—

the clear-cut. Was she out here at her cabin on the lake too? Had she come into our cabin while we were skinny-dipping and taken the phone? But that was crazy. She was an old lady. Besides, what would be the point?

"It'll turn up," Galen said. "I'm starving. Come on, let's eat."

We had hot dogs and canned beans for dinner, cooked on the word-burning stove. There was no running water, so when we were done, we stacked the dirty pots and dishes in the sink.

After that, Mia, Galen, and Liam had to rub antibacterial ointment on their tattoos, so I went around the room lighting the candles and kerosene lanterns.

Then Mia broke out some bottles of beer that her older brother had bought for her, and we all gravitated back to the fireplace. Galen and Mia sat on the sofa together, and Liam and I took the chairs on either side. I couldn't help but notice that Liam sat in the chair as far from Galen as possible.

"Hey, let's play Three Truths and a Lie," Mia said.

This was a party game I'd played a couple of times before. A person has to make four different statements about himself, and the rule is that three of the statements have to be true and one is a lie. Then the others try to guess which is which. I'm not really into games, but it was better than being reminded again how I was the only one who didn't have a matching tattoo.

Galen had never played before. When Mia finished explaining the rules, he said, "What's the point?"

"To see how good a liar you are!" Mia said. "We keep score. If anyone manages to pick out the lie, they get a point. And if anyone thinks a truth is a lie, then . . . wait. Who gets a point then?"

"The person whose turn it is," Galen said.

"Right! See? You already got it!" She laughed. She'd just started drinking, but she was already a little tipsy. "Who wants to go first?"

"I will," I said. I was all about living in the here and now, right? "But I need to think for a second."

As I was thinking, I thought I heard Mia sigh impatiently, but it turned out to be her opening another bottle of beer.

"Okay, I've got it," I said. I paused for maximum effect. "I won a contest in the first grade by reading the most books in a single year."

"Truth!" Mia said.

"Why do you say that?" Galen said.

"Because it's the first statement by the first player in the whole game. No one ever begins Three Truths and a Lie with a lie."

I tried to hide my annoyance with a noncommittal smile, but she was right.

"Okay, number two," I said. "I once found a fingernail in a can of soup."

Galen looked at Liam, but he just shrugged.

"It's another truth," Mia said.

"How do you know?" Galen said.

"I just do."

Mia was right again. Maybe it was a piece of onion, but it sure looked like a fingernail.

I leaned back in my chair. "I have six computer passwords. The most complicated one, for really important stuff, is banger98fg. And if it's case-sensitive, the R and the G are both capitalized."

"Lie," Mia said.

And yes, she was right again. This was my lie. I did have six passwords, but the one I'd recited wasn't one of them—I'd just made it up. Tipsy or not, Mia was good at this.

"I'm not even done yet," I protested. "Can I at least finish all four statements before you decide which one is which?"

Mia waved me onward. "Go on, go on!"

But she'd already rattled me with her uncanny lie detection. And I'd already told my lie, so I had to come up with another truth.

Finally I said, "I did my seventh grade science fair project on solar energy."

Almost instantly, Mia said, "Truth! The third one is the lie. The computer password."

"I hate to say it," Galen said, "but I agree with Mia."

Liam gave me an apologetic grimace, then nodded.

I sank deeper into my seat. "Okay, okay, you all got me. I suck at this."

"You don't suck," Mia said. "You're just a terrible liar."

How was being a terrible liar not the same thing as sucking? Wasn't that the whole point of the game?

"Seriously," I said, "how was I so obvious?"

"Well, for one thing, you have a tell," Mia said.

"A what?" I don't know why I was offended, but I was.

"Something people do when they lie, but they're not aware they're doing it. Almost everyone has one. Some people blink more than normal or cross their arms. You lean back, sort of trying to prove to people you're relaxed, that you're *not* lying."

"I do not," I said. But even as I said this, I realized that maybe I did.

"There's one more thing," Mia said. "A lie's usually longer than a truth. People go on and on, offering more and more detail. They think lots of detail will convince others it's the truth—or maybe convince themselves. Most people get nervous when they lie, so they have to sort of talk themselves into it. People use fewer words to tell the truth because it *is* the truth. They don't need to dress it up or play games with themselves."

I thought about the lie I'd told. Mia was right: I'd added that stuff about why some of my computer passwords are more difficult, and that the letters are sometimes case-sensitive, to make it sound more true. Is that why it had sounded false?

"I had no idea this was so complicated," I said.

Mia laughed. "Are you kidding? The difference between a truth and a lie, that's just about the most complicated thing in the whole world."

"But now that you've told us all your secrets, you've given up your advantage," Liam said.

"*Have* I?" she said, smiling mysteriously. "The only real secret is being able to read people, to really listen to exactly what it is they're saying. And that's a skill that can't be taught."

Liam blew her a raspberry, and Galen threw a beer bottle cap at her.

At the same time, someone coughed in the yard outside.

"What was that?" I said, sitting up straighter.

"What was what?" Mia said.

"Didn't you hear that? It sounded like a cough. Outside."

"It was probably an animal," Mia said. "They make some weird noises, trust me."

"It wasn't an animal," I said. "It was a person."

"I didn't hear anything," Galen said.

I wanted Liam to back me up, to say he'd heard the sound

too, but he just stared at me. I guess he hadn't heard it either.

"I'll go," Galen said, meaning the game.

"Go for it," Mia said.

But I got up and walked to the door, opened it, and looked outside. The darkness surprised me. The stars blazed in the sky, but that just made the lake and the rain forest in front of me look impossibly black. The last time I'd looked, it had still been dusk. The outside air was cool and wet—a sharp contrast to the stuffy, sooty air inside the cabin—but the only sounds I heard were the quiet gurgle of the lake and the irregular dripping of water from the trees.

"Close the door," Mia said. "It's cold."

"I could swear I heard someone," I said.

"Maybe it's the neighbors out for a walk," Mia said. "There's a cabin farther up the lake, remember?"

"Mrs. Brummit? Wouldn't we have heard her car?"

"It's not just her. She has a big family. They don't all come up here at the same time."

A big family? Could one of them have taken our phone? But it was clear that no one else was thinking this, so I felt stupid saying it. We didn't even know for a fact the phone was gone. We'd probably misplaced it.

I closed the door and returned to the others.

"I once rode Space Mountain at Disneyland with the lights on." This was Galen, the first part of his turn. He didn't blink or cross his arms or lean back. He'd barely moved at all. We'd all been watching.

We all looked at Mia, but she hesitated.

"I . . . don't know," she said. "That could be true."

"I didn't know what 'kitty-corner' meant until six months ago," Galen said. Once again, he hadn't moved at all.

And once again, Liam and I looked to Mia for guidance.

"Okay, *this* is how it's done," she said, and I couldn't help but be a little offended. I mean, she was obviously referring to me.

Galen moved now, but only to wiggle his ass a little. "I'm not wearing any underwear right now," he said.

Liam's face reddened even in the flickering firelight. Mia laughed.

"And last but not least," he said, "I once invented something that ended up being used by millions of people."

"Seriously?" I said.

Galen smiled obliquely. Is that the right word? Obliquely? I think so.

Mia said, "Oh fuck, very clever!"

"What is?" Liam asked.

"That last one," she said. "About inventing something used by millions of people? That totally sounds like a lie. Which means it's *not* the lie. It's a truth." She gave Galen a respectful salute. "Clever strategy."

"But how could Galen have invented something that's used by millions of people?" Liam said. "Wouldn't you know?"

"I'm tellin' ya," Mia said. "It's a truth. Don't fall for it."

"Well?" Galen said, leaning forward on the seat, defiantly staring us down, even Mia, who was right next to him. "What's the verdict?"

The three of us thought about everything Galen had said. He hadn't given us much to go on. Had he put his boxers back on when he'd gotten dressed after skinny-dipping? I'd been focused on Liam at that point, worried about how embarrassed he was, so I hadn't been looking. And Mia had dressed before Galen and was already walking to the cabin. None of us had seen.

"I think he rode Space Mountain with the lights on," I said. "That one definitely sounds true."

"And I can definitely see him not knowing what 'kitty-corner' means," Liam said. This was a thinly veiled insult, but Galen sort of deserved it.

"Sometimes he does go commando," Mia mused.

"So," Galen said, "is that your guess? The underwear one is the lie?"

"No," Liam said. "It's the invention thing. How could it not be?"

I nodded, agreeing with Liam. That had to be it.

"I *told* you guys," Mia said. "That's not it." She turned to Galen, trying to undress him with her eyes—something I was too embarrassed to do. "Nope," she said. "I say it's the underwear one."

Galen stood up and unbuttoned the top of his pants.

"Take it off! Take it off!" Mia said. Now she was something more than tipsy.

Bumping and grinding, Galen lifted his shirt and slowly slid his unbuttoned jeans down. He *definitely* wasn't wearing any underwear. He flashed us more than a hint of his light brown pubes before tugging his pants up again, laughing.

"Noooo!" Mia said. "You're such a fucking tease!"

Liam shifted in his chair.

"So if that was a truth," I said, "which one was the lie?"

Galen did his own dramatic pause. Part of me wanted to strangle him with his grin.

Then he announced, "Space Mountain. I've never been to Disneyland at all. But I saw this video once where they rode it with the lights on, and I could tell it was supposed to be a big deal."

"Wait," Liam said. "So it's a truth that you invented something that was used by millions of people? What did you invent?"

"The watering gun," Galen said.

"The what?" Mia said.

"It's the spout of a watering can attached to a big squirt gun, like a Super Soaker. You use it to water hanging plants that are too high for a watering can and too far for a hose."

"I think I've seen that in stores," Liam said. "You invented that?"

"In the fifth grade. For my mom, when her hanging fuchsias started dying."

"So you're rich?" I asked.

"He didn't say that," Mia said.

I was confused.

"I didn't say that it was *my* invention you see in the stores," Galen said, and Mia nodded knowingly. "What I *said* was I invented something that ended up being used by millions of people. And I did. I invented the watering gun. And then someone else invented the same damn thing, and they ended up getting rich. Then again, I never showed my invention to anyone except my mom. And I was only using duct tape."

I had to admit, this was pretty clever—both as an invention and as a strategy to play the game.

But Liam said to Mia, "Is that fair?"

"Absolutely," Mia said. "Everything he said was literally true. We—or I should say *you*—just jumped to the wrong conclusion. But that's exactly how the game is played. I *love* it when truths are only true from a certain point of view."

Liam clenched his jaw.

"Really good one!" Mia said to Galen. "You're a great liar. I'll keep that in mind the next time I ask if you've ever cheated on me."

He kicked back on the sofa, and I couldn't help but notice that the top of his pants was still unbuttoned. "I'll keep it in mind the next time I *do*."

Now she threw a bottle cap at him.

"Mia," Liam said, "your turn."

She grinned like the villain in some Disney cartoon, like she'd been waiting for this moment all night. She probably had been.

She paused for a second, then said, "I *am* wearing underwear."

We all laughed. Was this the truth? Who knows? When she'd been getting dressed, Galen had been facing the lake shaking his junk at Liam and me, so she was the *last* place the rest of us had been looking.

"I've never seen any of the *Star Wars* movies," Mia said.

"Not even the new one?" I said.

"Nope."

"Whoa," Galen said.

"I don't shave my legs very often, but when I do, I also wax my upper lip," Mia said. "If I didn't, you'd probably be able to see my mustache. No, you'd *definitely* be able to see my mustache."

"That one had a lot of detail," Galen said. "Which means it could be the lie."

"Except that Mia just told us how lies supposedly use more detail," Liam pointed out. "Which means she was probably setting us up. Which means it's a truth."

This is *complicated,* I thought.

"Well, I agree with the part about her not shaving her legs very often," Galen said. "That part's *definitely* true."

"Fuck you," Mia said, and Liam laughed.

"Hold on," I said to Mia. "Don't you have one more?"

Mia glanced toward the window in the kitchen. It was too dark to see anything outside now, so it was just this rectangle of blackness reflecting back the candles and lanterns inside the cabin. She took another swallow of beer and said, very quietly, "I think I killed someone when I was thirteen years old."

It sounded like—well, a drunken confession. Is that what it was? What had Mia said before? That you just had to *listen* if you wanted to know if something was true or not? This one sure *sounded* true.

For a second, no one said anything. It was so quiet you could hear the trees dripping in the forest outside.

"Are you kidding?" Liam asked.

"Am I kidding that we're playing Three Truths and a Lie, and I just said something that might be a truth and might be a lie?" She shook her head. "Fuck no!" Her demeanor had shifted again. Now she didn't sound like she was making a confession. Now she sounded like she was playing a stupid party game, and she was getting impatient the rest of us weren't playing along.

But that didn't change anything for Liam, Galen, and me. We all sat there. Outside, the trees continued to drip, but the dripping actually sounded slower now, even more sporadic than before. If I didn't know any better, I'd say that time itself had somehow slowed down.

Could Mia really be telling the truth about the fact that she'd killed someone? Maybe it had slipped out because she'd been drinking. Or maybe this was another example of what Galen had pulled: saying something so incredible that it sounds like a lie, only to have it be true from a certain point of view. But how did you "kill" someone from a different point of view? "Someone" definitely implied it was a person. Was the loophole that she only *thought* she'd killed someone? But what difference would that make?

"Um, can we ask a follow-up question?" Liam said.

"Fuck no!" Mia said. "Come on, come on, make your guesses." Now she sounded irritated.

Outside, the dripping was faster again, like time was back to normal.

"I think it's the second one," Galen said quietly. "*Star Wars*."

"You do?" I said, surprised. It's not that this was such an incredibly unlikely lie for Mia to tell. It's that if number two was a lie, that meant he thought number four had to be true.

Galen winked at me. "Nah! I think it's number four."

It was my turn to guess, but I didn't know what to say. I could say anything and Mia would have to tell us the truth, if the last one was a lie or not. But I guess some part of me wasn't sure I wanted to know.

"The fourth one," I said quickly. "That's the lie." Mia was simply a good actor, and she'd been setting us up with everything she'd said before.

Naturally, Liam nodded, agreeing with me.

What does it mean when you say there's a "pregnant" pause? When there's a pause full of anticipation and expectation, right? That's what this was.

Mia wiped her lips.

Then she burst out laughing. "Oh my God, you should see you guys' faces! You really think I *killed* someone! Of course that's the fucking lie!"

I felt stupid. Mia *had* tricked us.

Or had she? If the point was to get us to think a lie was the truth, it hadn't worked; not a single one of us had gone for it. Unless that's not what she'd been doing. Maybe it *had* been a genuine drunken confession. Or maybe she had some deeper agenda. Maybe this whole dumb party game

73

was some kind of mind game, like Galen teasing Liam out by the lake.

Liam had some fun friends, huh?

I scanned the room. Everyone was smiling except me. Galen twisted open another beer. Liam's admiration for Mia was obvious on his face.

"How could you have never seen any *Star Wars* movies?" Galen asked.

"It's because my brother loves them so much," Mia said. "I'm not watching them to piss him off."

"That sounds healthy," Liam said.

"Doesn't it?" Mia said. "Okay, whose turn is it now? Liam?"

I stood up and walked to the door again.

"Hey, I have a *Star Wars* joke," Galen said. "A guy walks into a droid bar and the bartender says, 'We don't serve your kind in here!'"

Galen stared at us with a big grin on his face, but no one laughed.

"It's a joke," Galen said.

"I figured," Mia said. "I don't get it."

"Of course you don't get it," Galen said. "You've never seen *Star Wars*. It's a line from the first movie. They go into the bar in Mos Eisley, and the bartender says about the droids, 'We don't serve their kind in here.' Only this is a droid bar, so they say it about *people*. See?"

"I guess," Mia said, barely smiling.

I opened the door and looked outside.

"Did you get it?" Mia said to Liam.

"Yeah," Liam said. "I just didn't think it was funny." Liam finally had Galen on a hook and was determined to make him squirm.

Standing at the open door, I said, "Ha! And you guys said there wasn't anyone out here!"

"Really?" Mia said. "Who's there?"

"Hey there!" I said, calling out into the yard. "Isn't it kind of late to be going for a walk?" I turned to Mia and the others. "He looks friendly enough."

"Really?" Mia said, even as she and the others stood up to see who I was talking to.

I stood aside as they gathered in the doorway. But a second

later, everyone turned to me. They hadn't seen anyone out in the darkness. There wasn't anyone there.

Confused, Mia said, "What's going on?"

It was finally my turn to smile mysteriously. "Nothing," I said, mostly to Mia. "Just proving that maybe I'm not such a terrible liar after all."

The sex with Liam that night was incredible.

That's too much information, isn't it? Well, I already told you about the skinny-dipping. Besides, it ends up being kind of important to the story.

At first I thought it was the fact that we had actual privacy for the first time since we'd started dating—or at least all the privacy that a sleeping loft allows. There was no way either my or Liam's parents were going to walk in on us way out here at this cabin in the rain forest.

But it was something else too. Something that's embarrassing to admit.

It was Galen. I kept remembering what he'd looked like naked down at the lake, or even with his jeans tugged partway down when he was doing that striptease. It didn't take me long to realize that Liam was thinking about Galen too. It was something about how often he was closing his eyes, and how he would sometimes stop and listen to the noises Galen and Mia were making in the bedroom—the squeaking of their bed, Galen's moans and grunts. Or maybe it was how passionate, even angry, Liam was. Somehow I knew he was totally pissed off at Galen even as he was also completely turned on by him. I know this should've upset or offended me, that he was thinking about someone other than me, but it didn't. It turned me on. I don't know if it's ever this way in straight sex—I've never *had* straight sex—but there was some kind of weird, unspoken feedback loop going on between the two of us, the way we were both turned on by the same thing, this thing that wasn't quite right. But we were giving in to it, surrendering to the mutual, wordless desire, which was pushing us both to greater and greater heights of urgency and passion.

Before long, we were slick with sweat, and I couldn't tell the difference between the pounding of Liam's heartbeat and my own. But no matter what we did, no matter how we explored and used each other's bodies, we couldn't find satisfaction, at least not for long. We kept waking up and going at it all over again, doing things we'd never done before, things I knew I'd be embarrassed about the next morning.

That's the one thing no one ever really tells you about sex. That it can sort of take you over. Most people say sex is healthy, that it's part of what it means to be a human being, and that's true. But there's another side. Sometimes you can lose yourself, and afterward, it's a little scary to realize you're not the person you thought you were.

I woke up the next morning to the sound of pancakes sizzling and the smell of batter on a hot skillet.

I groaned and rolled over, looking down from the sleeping loft. The cabin was so much brighter than the night before, even from just two windows—the one in the kitchen and one in the dining area directly under the sleeping loft. Only now did I realize there were no curtains.

"Morning, asshole!" Mia said, looking up at me from the stove. She was the one making pancakes.

How was it, I wondered, that she'd managed to fire up the

stove and mix the batter, but it wasn't until it had actually hit the skillet that I'd finally woken up? It was something about that particular sound and smell.

Next to me in bed, Liam moaned, and I realized I was naked. I pulled the sheet and blanket up, trying to cover myself even though I knew Mia couldn't see me all the way up in the loft.

"What time is it?" Liam said, rubbing his face.

"It's *morning*," Mia said. "Time has no meaning up at Moon Lake." You'd never have known it from school, but Mia was apparently a morning person. Liam and I were not, even on those mornings when we hadn't been up all night.

"If time has no meaning," Liam said, "you won't mind if I go back to sleep for another three hours." He rolled over toward the wall, taking most of the sheet and blanket with him. But I knew there was no going back to sleep for me now, not with the smell of those pancakes filling the cabin.

"I know why you're so tired," Mia said.

I blushed redder than I'd ever been. I knew I'd be embarrassed by what Liam and I had done the night before, but I hadn't expected to be *this* embarrassed. How loud had we been anyway? We'd definitely gotten carried away at times. And if we'd been able to hear Mia and Galen, they'd probably been able to hear us too. But even if Mia had heard, she had no way of knowing what we'd both been thinking.

"Where's Galen?" I said, attempting to change the subject. But as soon as I said it, I realized I hadn't really changed the subject at all.

"He went to take a shit," Mia said.

Lovely, I thought. I hoped Liam had heard her say that. For some reason, I wanted him to realize how crude his best friend could be. But he'd already buried his head back under a pillow.

I lay back, staring up at the ceiling. There were spiderwebs in the crannies, lots of them. We hadn't gotten them all the day before, like I'd thought.

A moment later, Galen came back inside and said, "We have a problem."

"You're right," Mia said. "I could swear I packed syrup." Something else she'd forgotten.

"Someone knocked over the outhouse."

"What?" Mia said.

"Go look."

This was definitely something I wanted to see for myself. I pulled on my clothes and followed Mia out into the yard.

It wasn't raining now, but it had during the night. It must've been after Liam and I had finally fallen asleep. The ground was even soggier than before—now it was like walking on a *wet* sponge—and the road was muddier too. The sky was overcast, but not quite gray. You couldn't tell if the rain clouds were coming or going.

The outhouse was a total wreck. The whole thing had been pretty simple—hardly more than four wooden walls and a roof around a box with a toilet seat over a pit in the ground. The box with the seat on it was more or less intact. That was good, because at least it meant nothing had spilled. And we still had a bathroom of sorts.

But the rest of it? It was a total mess, like a house after a tornado. The wood of the outhouse was really old, so when it had hit the ground, a lot of it had split and crumbled. That also meant there was no easy way of reassembling the thing.

I sensed Liam standing behind me. He must've heard us talking and followed us out of the cabin. He was buttoning his pants.

Mia stared at the wreckage. "Who would do this?" she said.

"Last night," I said. "Remember that cough I heard? I told you there was someone out here. I wasn't lying about that."

"Hold on," she said. "I used this thing hours after you heard that. Didn't we all? Before we went to bed? It was fine then."

"Who's to say the person kicked it over then," I said. "Maybe they did it later. After we went to bed."

"So this person hung out in the middle of a rain forest for a couple of hours? At night? Waiting around until we knocked off so they could tip over our outhouse?"

I guess she had a point, but did she have to be such a bitch about it?

I was about to remind everyone about the missing phone when Liam said, "Who's to say it was a person who knocked it over? Couldn't it have been an animal? Like a bear."

A bear? I thought.

"Why would a bear knock over an outhouse?" Mia said. But I could hear a note of concern in her voice.

"Are there any tracks?" Liam asked.

This seemed like a good question, but the only tracks I saw in the moss were from all of us, traipsing back and forth to the outhouse all night.

Galen held up a couple of the rotten planks, trying to piece them together like a puzzle. "What if it wasn't anyone or anything?" he said. "What if it fell over on its own?"

"Why would it do that?" I asked.

"Well, look at this wood," Galen said. "How rotten it is. And all this moss on the roof."

"That's a pretty big coincidence," Liam said. "I mean, no one from Mia's family comes out here for years, and then the weekend we do, the outhouse just happens to collapse?"

Liam was still annoyed with Galen from the day before.

But Galen didn't seem to notice. "Maybe that's what did it," he said. "Maybe it was ready to go, and whoever shut the door last, that's what made it finally topple over."

What Galen was saying made sense. Plus, it was a more

comforting theory than mine, the one about someone lurking in the woods. It was also more comforting than the theory about the bear, something even Liam seemed to concede.

So that was that. The Mystery of the Tipped-Over Outhouse had been solved. And for the time being, none of us gave it another thought.

7

"So what do we *do* up here?" Galen asked, back in the cabin, waiting for a fresh round of pancakes. The ones from before were stone cold now, but everyone says you need to toss the first few away anyway.

"Here at the cabin?" Mia said. "All kinds of things."

"Like . . . ?"

"Go fishing."

"We didn't bring any equipment."

"Go swimming."

"Tried that. Froze our balls off."

"Go for a hike."

Even Galen couldn't think of an objection to that.

"There's a really great view from the top of the hill on the other side of the lake," Mia said. "The hike's a bitch, but it's worth it."

• • •

It's strange using an outhouse with no walls. You can't help but feel really exposed. I guess it's because you *are* really exposed. You're about as vulnerable as a person can be.

It was after breakfast, and we were all taking a turn at the outhouse, with everyone else sort of agreeing to wait inside the cabin. When it was my turn, I sat there looking around at the wreckage of the fallen walls, and I couldn't help but wonder again if there really was someone up there in the woods with us. I thought I'd heard that cough outside the night before.

Except I was just being an idiot. The only people I had to worry about were Mia or Galen sneaking up on me, and that seemed like too much even for them. I was freaking myself out again, the way I'd done in Marot.

Later, the four of us set out for the trail Mia had talked about. The trailhead started just up the road from the cabin.

"I'm surprised there are still trails up here," I said. "Who would ever come this far in to go on a hike? And how would they get past that gate at the start of the logging road?"

"It started out as a hiking trail, but now it's probably an animal trail," Mia said. "Deer and goats and elk. They use trails too, you know."

But once again, Mia had forgotten about the clear-cut. Five minutes into the trail, the rain forest fell away and we were standing right at the edge of it.

"Fuck," Mia said. "Well, that was stupid of me."

It was weird being so close to the clear-cut, having it be right in front of me. From a distance, it had looked like total devastation. Even from the car on the way in, these clear-cuts had looked like nothing but a wasteland of churned dirt and twisted stumps littered with the skeletons of long-dead branches.

Closer now, I saw it wasn't lifeless. There were little trees growing up around the stumps—saplings or seedlings, I'm not sure which, a foot or more high. They looked fresh and bright with lots of new spring growth on the tips of their branches. Meanwhile, the old stumps and branches were slowly rotting away. It made me happy, knowing a new forest was rising even as the old one faded away. After a while, you might not even know the clear-cut had happened at all, not unless you looked really closely or knew a lot about forests.

It was almost enough to get me to forget what Mia had said during that stupid game the night before, about how she'd killed someone when she was thirteen. She'd said it was a lie, and it probably was—Mia trying to screw with us all—but it unsettled me even now.

Galen started up the trail in front of us, right into the clear-cut. "Who cares if they cut down some trees?" he said. "Hey, the view will still be the view, right?"

"Yeah," Liam muttered, "it's all about the destination, not the journey."

The rest of us followed behind Galen, hiking single file. Liam and I were bringing up the rear, and after a while we fell back a bit, so we could finally talk without the others over-hearing.

"You having fun?" I asked him.

"Sure," he said, but I could tell he was unsettled too. For him, it had to do with the skinny-dipping, with how Galen had treated him the night before—and probably how Galen was acting even today. Liam didn't like Galen, and not just because he was a total tease.

"What about you?" Liam asked me.

"Huh?"

"Are *you* having fun?"

"Sure."

"Rob, what is it?" He could tell there were things I wasn't saying either.

"It's nothing."

"Come on."

I hiked in silence for a moment.

"That game last night was something," I said at last.

"Three Truths and a Lie? What about it?"

"I just wondered what you thought about that thing Mia said."

Liam laughed.

"What?" I said.

"I knew you were going to bring that up."

"You did? Why?"

"I don't know. I just did."

"You don't think it was weird?" I asked.

"It was Mia," he said. "For Mia, weird is normal."

We hiked on in silence again. Rocks skittered under Liam's feet.

"I think she was telling the truth," I said.

He laughed again. "That she killed someone when she was thirteen years old?"

"Fine, forget it."

"No! No, I'm sorry. I shouldn't have laughed. Why do you think she was telling the truth?"

"Well, for one thing, she *sounded* like she was."

"But that's the whole point of the game. To sound like you're telling the truth even though you're not."

I thought about saying how it hadn't worked, that if Mia had meant to trick us, we'd all voted that as the lie anyway, but I was eighty-five percent sure Liam wouldn't listen. I decided to go right to the big guns.

"She *wasn't* wearing underwear," I said.

"What?"

"Don't you remember? She said she was wearing underwear—it was one of her truths. But it *wasn't* a truth. At one point, she bent over, and I didn't see the waistband of any underwear. She must not have put them back on after skinny-dipping. And she definitely wasn't wearing a bra, that was obvious." This was all true. I'd wanted to tell Liam ever since I'd noticed it the night before. But it hadn't felt right telling him with Mia in the cabin, and we'd had other things on our minds after going to bed.

"So what if she wasn't wearing any underwear?" Liam said.

I stopped on the trail and turned to face him.

"What?" he said.

"Do you really not see?" I asked. "That thing about her underwear was supposed to be her lie. The thing about killing someone—I don't think she meant to tell us that. I think it slipped out, maybe because she was drunk, or maybe because she finally wanted to tell someone. I think when she said it, she meant it to be true." I was a little annoyed that I had to explain all this. Whatever happened to our always knowing what the other was thinking?

92

"Unless she was wearing underwear and you just didn't see it. Think it through."

"Okay," I admitted. "That's a possibility." I started forward on the trail again.

"Or maybe the thing about the underwear was supposed to be her lie, but then she said that thing about killing someone because she wanted to screw with us. To shock us, you know? So she told two lies. I mean, come on, this is Mia." Liam could have been right about this too. "Or maybe she wanted to shock *you*," Liam went on, "because she senses you don't like her."

"*What?*" I said. "What are you talking about? I like Mia!"

Liam laughed. "Mia was definitely right about one thing last night. You're a *terrible* liar."

The closer we got to the top of the hill, the more amazing the view became. You could already see out our little valley or basin or whatever, into the area beyond. The clear-cuts weren't like squares on a patchwork quilt or anything like that. They seemed more random, and sometimes really oddly shaped. But they had to have a pattern of some sort. I figured it would all make more sense from the top of the hill when I could finally see the big picture.

As for the lake below, it really was like the moon, almost perfectly round. It was also interesting how it was surrounded by rain forest on one side and a clear-cut on the other. Two halves more or less evenly divided. It was like two warring armies about to meet in battle. I stared down at it all, trying to make out which army had the advantage, which one was winning the war.

That's when I noticed that, far below us, someone had set our cabin on fire.

8

The four of us went down that hill a lot faster than we'd gone up. We'd been hiking for almost two hours, but we made it back to the lake in fifteen minutes flat.

The cabin wasn't on fire. Everything looked perfectly fine, both inside and out.

So what did we see?

"I don't get it," Mia said, still out of breath from the run. "There was fire. And smoke. We all saw it."

"I can still smell it," Galen said.

I smelled it too. Woodsmoke. But that could have been the lingering smell of the fire we'd made to cook breakfast that morning, or even campers somewhere nearby in the woods.

We walked all the way around the cabin, but nothing was burning or even charred. Honestly, it was so wet and covered with moss that I had a hard time believing it would have burned even if it *was* set on fire.

"Look," Mia said. She was staring at the rusted metal barrel in the yard. Wisps of smoke rose from inside. We'd missed it before, because we'd all been so focused on the cabin. She and Galen walked closer and peered inside.

"Someone lit a fire in here," Galen said.

Liam and I looked inside too. Sure enough, there were smoldering embers at the bottom of the bin. Someone had lit a fire, but it had burned out. It must have mostly been newspapers and kindling, something that would burn big and bright, but not for long. From the top of the hill, it might even have looked like the cabin was on fire.

"Okay," Mia said. "This is too weird."

"What's this for anyway?" Galen asked, gesturing to the bin.

"We used to use it to burn garbage."

"Why would it be on fire now?"

Mia shook her head. "I have absolutely no idea."

"What about the Brummits?" I said. "Would they use it?"

She shrugged. "I guess it's possible. But I don't remember

them ever doing that before. And it seems strange that they wouldn't even ask."

We all stood there, not moving. The moss squished under someone's feet, but I wasn't sure who it was.

"You know," Mia said, "I think maybe we should go pay a friendly visit to the Brummits."

Mia said the other cabin wasn't far—a quarter of a mile or so down the dirt road. We decided to walk.

Before long, we were deep inside the rain forest again. But as we kept walking, the forest changed around us. It wasn't like all the rain forest we'd seen before.

It was a bog. And suddenly we'd gone back even further in time: if the rain forest had felt like something from a million years ago, this place was like something from millions of years before that. I half expected to see a dinosaur.

Fir trees had been replaced by fast-growing alders with bushy branches and emerald leaves. They rose up out of pools of muck, clawing for sunlight against the trees crowded around them. In the pools, jade-colored algae grew in swirls under the water's surface, reminding me of distant galaxies. The moss still hung heavy off the trees, but the ferns had given way to swamp cabbages, the pointed yellow spikes of their flowers just beginning to unfurl. Deeper in the swamp, I saw devil's walkingstick, a tall plant with twisty stalks and branches, and ridiculously sharp thorns.

Water still dribbled down from above, but now it landed in stagnant pools, not on vegetation, so each droplet made a muffled *plink*, like the sound of a hundred leaky faucets. I smelled moss and methane, blooming flowers and rotting leaves. The whole area somehow managed to smell both clean and dirty at the same time. It was funny that my first impression was that it seemed older than the rest of the rain forest, like we'd gone back to the time of dinosaurs, because the trunks of the trees weren't nearly as thick here. It was clearly a much newer forest. But maybe that's what made it seem more alien. The fact it was so new, so changeable. In this time, the whole world was fresher. In this place, evolution had only just started. Everything was still in flux and anything was possible.

I stared over at the lake itself, barely visible through the new spring foliage on the trees. It wasn't clear to me where that lake ended and this bog began—if the lake just flowed through the trees into the swamp, or if there was some kind of beachlike buffer. But at least the dirt road was high enough above the water level that it wasn't any muddier than usual.

Until it *was* muddy. The road must've dipped down, because the water suddenly seeped out in front of us, and then we were trying to navigate through muddy pools. We were mostly okay if we stayed on the bulge in the middle of the road. Here it was covered with grass.

"It's only like this in the spring," Mia said. "The level of the lake is higher. In the summer, the road is dry."

Mia had been right: the cabin itself wasn't far. And it was built on higher ground, so the bog soon fell away behind us and we were once again surrounded by fir trees. It was newer and bigger than Mia's parents' cabin, made of red cedar, not whatever dark, ancient wood Mia's grandparents had used. The neatly shingled roof was mostly free of moss too, which meant the cabin had nice clean lines, not lumpy, saggy ones. A pale green fiberglass rowboat sat overturned near the shore of the lake, and a flat inflatable, a kid's toy, drooped down in the crook of a tree. I couldn't tell if it was an inner tube or an animal or what.

But there were no cars parked outside.

"Maybe they left," Galen said. "Maybe they stopped at our cabin on the way out to burn their garbage."

"On a Saturday morning?" Liam said. "If they came all the way out here, wouldn't they stay for the weekend?" Liam pointed at the road. "And if there was someone staying here last night, wouldn't there be tire tracks?"

He was right. There were no fresh tire tracks, and any vehicle would have left some in the mud.

"Let's look inside," Mia said. When we stared at her, she added, "It's fine. We used to be really friendly."

Mrs. Brummit didn't seem very friendly the day before, I thought.

"Friendly enough that they'd use your fire bin without asking?" Liam asked.

Mia fluffed her hair. "That's the million-dollar question, isn't it?"

100

Unlike Mia's parents' cabin, this one had a small deck. The lawn furniture was frayed and weathered. When she tried the door, it was locked.

"I thought you said no one locks their doors up here," I said.

"No, I said *we* don't lock our door up here." She hesitated a second, then she knocked. That's probably what she should have done first.

No one answered.

We peered in through the curtainless windows, which were bigger than the ones in Mia's parents' cabin, but it was dark inside so we couldn't see anything.

"Come look at this," Galen said. He hadn't joined us on the porch. He was over by the outhouse. They didn't have plumbing either.

When the rest of us reached the outhouse, Galen pointed. There was a spiderweb on the crack between the door and the outhouse. It was ragged, like it was old, and spattered with morning dew.

He opened the door and peered down into the toilet itself, even inhaling to smell it.

"No one's been here in a long time," he said at last.

"Then who lit that fire?" Mia asked. "And knocked over our outhouse?"

"And who did I hear last night?" I said. I was back to being eighty percent sure it had been a person I'd heard out in the dark.

But of course no one had any answers.

I shivered. All around me, water trickled down from the moss in the trees. We were away from the bog again, so it didn't sound like the dripping of a hundred faucets. Even so, it was starting to annoy me.

"I think we should get back," Liam said.

No one disagreed.

We walked back along the road through the bog in silence. I was happy to finally leave it behind.

When we reached the cabin, Galen said, "A guy walks into a bar, and his gymnastics coach says, 'No, no, you're supposed to swing yourself *between* the parallel bars, not walk right into them!'"

Liam didn't laugh, but Mia did. It was like she and Galen

were going to pretend that nothing had happened. Someone was up in these woods with us, someone who didn't want to be seen, but Mia and Galen didn't even care.

This was the big downside of being with people who lived in the here and now. They gave hardly any thought to the past and they were too stupid to worry about the future, even when the future seemed like something you should definitely be worried about.

Once we were all inside the cabin, I said, "I think we should go."

Everyone looked at me.

"Go where?" Mia said.

"Home," I said. "Away. We can even spend the night in a motel somewhere along the road. I have money."

I knew Liam wouldn't laugh at me, but I thought Mia and Galen might, or at least look at me like I was crazy. They didn't. Everyone stared at me with eyes wide open.

This surprised me. Maybe they were scared too and had just been pretending they weren't. I couldn't help but wonder what else they might be pretending about.

"There's someone up here," I said. "I heard them last night. Whoever it was, they knocked over the outhouse and lit that fire. And they also stole our phone."

The missing phone. No one had mentioned that since the night before. It was one thing when it seemed like we'd misplaced it, but now that we knew we weren't alone, it meant something completely different. It meant that whoever was up here with us had stolen it and was trying to cut off our only means of contact with the outside world.

"It could be the Brummits," I said.

"You think the Brummits stole our satellite phone?" Mia said.

Now she looked at me like I was crazy.

"It's only a theory," I said. "But, I mean, it's possible."

"But why would they do it?"

"Maybe to jerk us around. Or maybe for something more."

"Something more like what?" Galen asked.

"Like they have something else planned, and they don't want us calling for help."

No one said anything for a second. Then Mia's eyes narrowed.

"They were angry at my parents and grandparents," she said. "Not me. Not *us*."

"Maybe," Liam said. "But maybe not." I smiled at him, grateful for the support. At least the two of us were in sync again.

"But there wasn't anyone over at their cabin," Mia said stubbornly. "There hasn't *been* anyone over at their cabin."

"Maybe it's not the Brummits," I said. "But we *know* someone else is up here. And there are all kinds of things they could have taken from this cabin. Expensive things, like our wallets and our cell phones. But the only thing they *took* was that satellite phone. Doesn't that mean they don't want us calling for help? And if that's true, doesn't it worry you about what they might have planned?"

Once again, no one said anything. We sat there thinking about it for maybe twenty seconds, frozen like trolls at daybreak.

Then we turned and started packing, all of us at exactly the same time. Maybe one of us had moved first—we probably had—but it didn't seem like it. We didn't talk any more about it either. It was like there wasn't anything left to discuss.

As we packed, I felt clearheaded and focused in a way I

hadn't felt all day, maybe not since we'd entered that little town of Marot the day before.

Five minutes after we started packing, Mia said, "I don't believe it. Look what I just found!"

She turned around from the kitchen, holding up the satellite phone.

"What the hell?" Galen said. "Where was it?"

"Behind the food in one of the cupboards. I must have put it up there by mistake."

Everyone stopped packing. Or rather they started *unpacking*. Again, it all went completely without saying. But this time, I hadn't joined them.

"Wait," I said. "Does that mean we're not leaving?"

Everyone looked at me.

"Why would we leave now?" Mia said.

"Well, the fire and the outhouse . . . ," I said. "I mean, there's still someone up here with us."

"Yeah, but if they didn't take our phone, what difference does it make? They burned some trash in our bin, and they accidentally knocked over the outhouse. So what?"

"But . . ." But what? She was right. The missing satellite phone was the big deal. The rest of it was just silly stuff. And now it turned out the phone hadn't been missing after all.

"But I did hear someone," I said. "Last night, right outside our cabin."

"I'm sure it was an animal," Mia said. "They can make some really strange noises. You'd be surprised how often they can sound like a person."

Maybe it was *an animal,* I thought. *But maybe it wasn't.* If it wasn't the Brummits, maybe it was those guys who'd chased us that night at the tattoo parlor. Maybe they'd somehow followed us all the way out to the Olympic Peninsula. But even as I thought this, I realized we would have seen them following behind us on the logging road, especially in the clear-cuts. Besides, Mia had locked the gate behind us.

Everyone was staring at me, trying to take me seriously, but I could see the little seedlings of impatience sprouting in their minds.

Galen scratched his wrist, the spiderweb tattoo. I looked

and saw the same one on Mia and Liam too. Going away for this weekend had been my idea—a way for the four of us to bond because I'd been feeling left out. Now here I was deliberately separating myself from them.

I was an idiot.

"You okay?" Mia asked me, and she sounded sincere.

"Yeah," I said, but I wasn't really. I was embarrassed. "I guess I sort of freaked myself out." Even now, I was expecting Mia to laugh at me, or make me feel stupid, but she didn't. Galen didn't either, which I appreciated.

"If someone really was out to get us, they wouldn't have just taken our phone," Galen said.

"What?" I said.

"Well, I mean, what about our car?"

I still didn't understand.

"He's right," Mia said. "What good would it do to take our means of communication unless they also cut off our means of escape?"

I thought about this for a second. Then I said, "You guys are just saying this *now*?"

Everyone laughed at my joke, and that made me feel good.

"So if you're still worried," Galen said, "let's go see if everything's okay with the car."

"No, it's fine. Really." The truth is I did want to check the car, but I was tired of feeling like a baby.

So I was really glad when Galen said, "Oh, come on. Now you've got *me* curious."

When we were out at the car, I held my breath as Galen slid the key into the ignition. I was ninety-eight percent sure that everything was going to be okay. But there was still that two percent.

He turned the key.

And the car started up just fine, no problem at all.

The car purred. No one said anything for a second.

And then we all busted up laughing—Galen in the driver's seat, and Mia, Liam, and me standing around outside. I guess I hadn't been the only one holding my breath, the only one worried about exactly what was going to happen.

It was kind of funny. Did we really think that someone was

terrorizing us? That night was going to fall and we were slowly going to be picked off one by one? We'd obviously seen too many slasher movies.

We all stood there laughing together. The sound of it echoed off the lake, and that's when I finally felt a real connection with Liam's friends. Ten minutes earlier, I'd been feeling the exact opposite, but something had changed. Now I knew they cared about me, that they saw me as part of their group. I didn't have a wrist tattoo, but maybe that didn't matter.

That's the point about surprising things, I guess. They really do happen when you least expect them.

The four of us spent the afternoon doing different things. Galen and Mia went off to try to rebuild the outhouse, their hammering echoing out across the stillness of the lake. Meanwhile, Liam and I found Mia's family's old rowboat and decided to take it out on the water.

"That was funny," Liam said as we paddled lazily around. "That thing with the car."

"Yeah," I said. I was still a little embarrassed by everything that had happened. I wanted to tell him that it had all been for the best, that I was actually starting to feel comfortable around Mia and Galen, but I wasn't sure how to put it into words.

"So you're finally starting to see why I'm friends with Mia."

I should've figured Liam would know what I was thinking.

Still, I said, "Why do you keep saying that? I like Mia."

"Oh Rob, stop. Terrible liar, remember?"

We both laughed and the boat rocked a little, just from our laughter. The air smelled like water again. Out on the lake, it was clean and fresh, not like the stink of that bog.

"Okay, okay," I said. "Maybe I didn't get her before. But I had my reasons. Like you and Galen."

"What about me and Galen?"

"Well, you don't like him either."

"What? That's not true."

"Seriously?" I said. "You might be a better liar than me, but you're not *that* much better."

Now only I laughed, and this time the boat didn't rock.

"Besides," I said, "you and Mia don't really have that much in common either."

"Sure we do. We both like pancakes. And *Game of Thrones*. And toasted marshmallows."

"That's not what I mean. I mean about the way you take on the world. She jumps in headfirst."

"And I don't?"

I raised an eyebrow.

"Okay, okay," he said. "But maybe that's what I like about her. She's different from me. She makes me do things I wouldn't necessarily do by myself." He hesitated. "Things like asking you out."

"You're kidding!" This was a surprise.

"No, I'm not. She totally pressured me into it. She was tired of me moaning about the fact that I didn't have a boyfriend. I mentioned I thought you were cute, and she wouldn't stop until I did something about it. She was the one who found out you were gay. She quizzed you one day in the hallway."

Was this true? I did have a vague memory of a conversation with a weird girl at school, someone I didn't even know suddenly all up in my face. That was Mia?

"But she never asked me if I was gay," I said. And I wouldn't have told her if she had.

"Yeah, but she knows how to read people."

So I had Mia to thank for the fact that Liam and I were even together?

"How did you meet her," I said, "back when you first became friends?"

Liam had to think about it. "I was sort of her tutor. She was always goofing off in class and had terrible grades, so a teacher asked me to help her with her math. As soon as we met together alone, I saw how smart she was. She knew the stuff, she just didn't like school. So she hid what she knew. She didn't want people to know who she really was. I liked that about her. Everyone had an idea of the kind of kid I was, and they were right. Even my coming out didn't surprise people. I didn't have any mystery at all. I was exactly the person you thought." He shrugged. "Maybe I still am. But maybe I'm not completely, because my best friend isn't the person you'd think it would be, is it?"

He had a point.

"I see what you got out of being friends with her," I said. "But what did she get out of being friends with you?"

"Thanks a lot!" He used the oar to splash me.

"You know what I mean," I said. "You said she didn't want people knowing she was smart. She wasn't worried about hanging out with you?"

"We had the perfect cover, being tutor and tutor-ee. No one knew we were actually friends. Not until a lot later."

"That doesn't really answer the question."

"Well, like I said, Mia's smart. She doesn't like being around stupid people. That's the problem with being a smart slacker— you get paired with all the idiots. But Mia wasn't an idiot. She was just bored."

"And it helped that you were gay," I said.

"What do you mean?"

"Well, there wasn't ever anything romantic between you. You were 'safe.'"

He thought about this. "Yeah. I mean, we had sex once. But still."

I did an actual double take. "What?"

"I told you that," he said. "Didn't I?"

"No! When did this happen?" When Liam had told me months ago that he'd had sex with one other person, I'd assumed he meant a guy.

"Oh jeez, forever ago," Liam said. "Maybe two years?"

Two years wasn't exactly *forever*. They would have been sixteen.

"How did it happen?" I said. "Whose idea was it?"

He laughed. "Who do you *think*?"

"And it was a disaster?" I said. "And afterwards you realized you were gay?"

"Oh, I'd already told her I was gay. And it wasn't a *disaster*. I mean, we did it, and it was fine."

"Wait. You already knew you were gay? And you *liked* it?"

Liam grinned. "I love that you're jealous."

Was I jealous? If I was, it was stupid.

"A little," I admitted. "Not that you guys had sex. That you had a secret I didn't know about."

He shrugged. "It's only a secret because I forgot to tell you."

By the time we got back to shore, Liam desperately needed to pee, so he hopped out of the boat and ran for the trees. I pulled the rowboat up alone.

"Hey, I'll help you," Mia said, trotting my way.

"Thanks," I said, and we pulled the boat back up where we'd found it, then covered it with a crusty plastic tarp.

"So what'd you think?" Mia said.

"Huh?" I said.

"Of the lake. Did you see Crow Island?"

"Crow Island?"

"Out on the lake."

"There's no island on the lake," I said.

"Sure there is." She pointed.

I looked to where she was pointing, but not that closely. If there was an island, wouldn't I have noticed it?

"Just *look*," she said.

I still didn't see anything. I was seventy percent sure she was trying to bullshit me. Maybe she hadn't accepted me into her circle after all.

"Close to shore," she said. She stepped closer to me and actually positioned my head so I was looking in the right direction. She was wearing some kind of fruity perfume—or maybe it was her shampoo—and I couldn't help but be reminded that she and Liam had once had sex. "It's hard to see up against the trees."

Then I saw it. It was on the far side of the lake and small—probably no more than ten feet across—but it was definitely there, lush and spilling over with trees and plants. That's how it blended so well into the background of the rain forest. But I hadn't noticed it from up on the hillside either. Sometimes we really do see only the things we expect to see.

"Wow," I said. "It's really there."

Mia laughed. "You thought I was lying?"

"No, I . . ." I didn't know how to answer. Not without lying myself.

"Even I can't invent an island out of thin air," she said. She was suddenly very serious. "That's the number one rule of lies. If you're going to tell one, make damn sure it's believable."

Later, when we were all back inside the cabin and getting ready for dinner, we realized there were no clean dishes left. Everything still needed to be washed from breakfast and dinner the night before, along with all the pots and pans.

I hadn't done any of the cooking, so I said, "I'll do it. At the well, right?"

Mia nodded, so I stacked as much as I could and carried it out to the pump.

There was a dingy white basin under the spout of the

pump, sort of a mini-bathtub. It was already full of water. Not just because we'd used the pump that weekend—the basin had been full of rainwater when we'd arrived.

The food had dried on the plates and pots, so I decided to soak them for a bit.

As I slipped the dishes into the water, I noticed something dark on the bottom of the basin—black and rectangular. The light was fading, but whatever it was stood out against the white porcelain. Like I said, I'd been using the pump all weekend, but I'd never noticed anything in the basin before.

I reached down to grab it. The water was icy against my skin, somehow much colder than the lake.

The second my fingers touched it, I realized what it was.

Our satellite phone.

The phone was worthless after being soaked in the water.

I brought it into the cabin and explained to the others where I'd found it.

"But that doesn't make any sense," Mia said. "How . . . ?"

It took everyone a second to sort of piece it together in

their minds. Someone had stolen our phone the night before while we were skinny-dipping, then somehow slipped it back in the cabin when we weren't looking, then stolen it *again* that afternoon and thrown it in the basin. Or maybe we really had misplaced it the night before, and then someone had stolen it that afternoon and thrown it in the water.

I wasn't sure which scenario was more unlikely.

"It's the Brummits," I said.

"No," Mia said. "That still doesn't make any sense."

"Who else could it be?"

"Anyone. Kids out mountain biking. People who live in the backcountry. My parents leave the cabin unlocked, so maybe someone's been up here using it, and they got upset when we showed up."

"I don't think so," Liam said. "Remember the rat poop on the floor? It was untouched."

"But the car . . . ," Galen said. "It was fine."

We all fell silent again. Earlier that afternoon, it had been fine, but was it still?

Galen grabbed the keys and turned for the door. Once

again, it seemed a lot darker outside than it had been only a few minutes earlier. Night had fallen like an ax.

Out at the car, Galen turned the ignition.

The car turned over.

And I was just about to start laughing like before, say to the others, "How paranoid are *we*?"

But it *kept* turning over. It never actually fired.

And no matter how many times Galen turned the ignition and pressed the gas, it never did.

The car wouldn't start.

11

Galen went back inside to get a flashlight. With it, he was able to tell that someone had punctured the gas tank. All the gasoline had soaked right into the ground. I don't know why we hadn't smelled it right away. Now that we knew it was there, the smell was overpowering. We'd all been so focused we hadn't even noticed.

"Those fuckers!" Mia said. "Those *fuckers*!"

"How'd they do it?" Liam said. "Wouldn't they have had to open the trunk or something?" We'd been dumb enough to leave the car unlocked, but even so, if someone had opened the trunk, wouldn't we have heard it? We hadn't left the area all afternoon, so wouldn't one of us have *seen* them?

"They could've reached underneath," Galen said. "With,

like, a small screwdriver or a nail. They'd have to know what they're doing, but it's possible." It was unsettling to hear Galen sound so serious, to not have him cutting corny jokes.

"What about footprints?" I said. But when we looked around with the flashlight, the only footprints we saw in the mud and moss were our own. I guess we'd walked over any other evidence that might've been there.

"Can it be fixed?" Liam asked.

"Do you smell that?" Galen said. "It's gasoline. Gasoline that should be in the tank that's now soaked into the ground. There's no way to get that gas back into the tank. And without it, we're screwed."

So we were stuck. Someone had cut off both our means of escape *and* our contact with the outside world. Were they still nearby? They could have been watching us even then.

"So what do we do?" Liam asked.

Mia was already staring at her cell phone, punching in numbers and listening even though there was no signal.

The rest of us went in to get our phones and tried them

too, moving to different places around the clearing. Galen even climbed up onto the roof of the car. But no matter what we did, there was no signal to be had.

"We should leave," Liam said. "Walk to the road."

"That's a long walk," Mia said. "Ten or fifteen miles."

"What else can we do? We can't stay here. Not with someone doing this."

But even as Liam said this, we all seemed to notice how dark it was—how it was already basically night.

"We could trip and fall," Mia said. "Or get lost. I only know this place in the light. I'm not sure I'd know the way out at night."

This was Mia talking, the person who always took stupid risks, leaping before she looked.

"So we just stay here?" I asked. Was that really our only option?

"Only until tomorrow morning," Galen said. "We'll lock the door. And stay together. And take turns keeping watch. Besides, we'll be safer here in this cabin than we would be out on the dirt road."

I looked at Liam in the glow of Galen's flashlight, at the

clench of his jaw, and I knew exactly what he was thinking: when had we voted to make Galen the leader?

But Galen was right and we both knew it. What else could we do?

No one felt much like playing Three Truths and a Lie that night. We didn't feel much like playing anything. But we had to do something after dinner, so we played cards. We started with hearts, then gin, then poker. But all those games require concentration, which none of us had much of, so we ended up playing game after game of War.

At some point, it started raining. We could hear the drops hitting the roof. Even through all that moss, it sounded like the patter of little mice. Then the rain came down faster, harder, so it sounded like squirrels, then deer. What kind of rainfall came after deer? Bears? Bigfoot? At what point did the roof collapse?

But as quickly as the rain had picked up, it lessened again. Back down to squirrels anyway.

"We should try to get some sleep," Galen said. "We have a long day ahead of us tomorrow."

Liam bristled, and I knew he was still annoyed by Galen taking charge.

"We should sleep in shifts," Liam said. "Keep watch."

"Good idea," Galen said.

"I'll stay up first," I said. "I'm not tired anyway."

To my surprise, Mia said, "I'll stay up with you."

I may have hesitated a little bit, but then I said, "Sure."

A few minutes later, Galen headed off to the bedroom, and Liam climbed up into the sleeping loft. I could hear him snoring almost right away. Then it was just Mia and me together, sitting on opposite chairs in front of the fire.

Neither of us said anything for a long time. We watched the fire, how the flames flickered unpredictably, and listened to the patter of rain on the roof.

"This is so fucked," she said at last.

"I know," I said. "But who expects stuff like this?"

"You want a beer?" She was already drinking one.

"It'll make me have to pee, and I'm not going outside," I said.

"Just use the bucket." No one was supposed to be alone tonight, so Galen had left a plastic bucket over by the door.

I knew Mia wouldn't have any problem using the bucket in front of anyone, but I wasn't so sure about me.

"That doesn't make me any more willing to have a beer," I said.

She laughed.

"I want cereal," she said, standing and walking to the kitchen.

"Now?"

"Cornflakes and shit. My comfort food." She poured herself a bowl, then added milk from the cooler. "And if there was ever a time I needed comfort, it's now, damn it."

I smiled.

She brought the bowl back to the sofa and ate it in front of the fire. She slurped something bad. It was kind of annoying.

"So," I said. "Galen."

"Oh, don't start," Mia said.

"What?"

"You're gonna say something bad."

"No, I like him. I do."

She brightened. "Really?"

I nodded.

"You just think he's hot," she said, still slurping.

I blushed. Why in the world had I brought up Galen?

"You *do*," she said. "I knew it! Been lusting after him all weekend."

"It's not like that," I lied.

"Oh please. And why not? He's fucking *hot*. You saw him when we were out skinny-dipping."

I wasn't sure whether to smile or roll my eyes. So I said, "Uh, let's just move on."

"Okay, but first you have to admit he's got a great ass."

"Mia." This time I did smile a little.

"Just admit it! Then we can talk about something else."

"Okay, okay," I said reluctantly.

"Okay *what*?"

"What you said."

"What did I say?"

"He has a great ass," I said, almost a whisper.

From the bedroom, Galen piped up, "You guys know I can hear everything you're saying, right?"

Now I was *beyond* embarrassed.

Mia called out, "You know you love it!"

"I'm flattered and humbled," Galen admitted.

Mia laughed, but I squirmed in my seat, beyond mortified.

After that Mia went to get more cornflakes, and I added wood to the fire and stirred up the embers, hoping I could restart this conversation the way I'd rekindled the fire.

A few minutes later, Mia checked on Galen.

"He's out," she said, quietly closing the door behind her. "Now we can say whatever the fuck we want."

"Yeah?" I said. "Great."

This time she sat right next to me on the sofa.

"Which is good," she said, "because there's something I wanted to ask you."

I tensed. I was certain she was going to ask me more about Galen—tell me she'd heard Liam and me up in the loft, and knew we were both lusting after him while having sex.

"Yeah?" I said quickly. "Because there's something I wanted to ask you too."

"Oh yeah?" she said casually. "About what?"

"That game we played last night." It was the only thing I could think of that would truly change the subject.

"What about it?" she said.

I hesitated. Did I really want to go through with this? Once I asked the question, I had to listen to whatever the answer was.

"You were telling the truth," I said. "Weren't you?"

"About what?" But I knew she was only pretending not to know what I was talking about. I guess I really had learned some lessons about lying.

I glared at her.

"You think I really killed someone?" she said.

"Well, it didn't sound like a lie when you said it. That's all."

"What did it sound like?"

I thought back. "A confession."

She finished the last of her cereal and set the bowl aside, then picked up her beer and sank into her corner of the couch. But she looked crammed in, stiff. Was that Mia's tell?

"Isn't that the whole point of the game?" she said. "To sound like you're telling the truth?"

"But your lie wasn't a lie at all. You *weren't* wearing underwear. Were you?"

She looked at me like she was seeing me for the very first time, like I had suddenly just materialized right before her eyes.

"Maybe I play the game differently than most people," she said. "Maybe I tell three lies and a truth. Maybe that's how I win the game."

"That would be cheating. Besides," I reminded her, "we weren't keeping score."

Mia's face was a mixture of smirks and grimaces. "Sounds like *someone* was." She looked around the cabin, and her expression turned wistful. "It's so weird being up here again. Everything is so familiar, but the last time I was up here, I was still a kid. The cabin is the same—well, it's more run-down, but it's *mostly* the same. But I'm completely different."

"I bet," I said, even as I realized she was changing the subject. I hadn't really wanted to talk about Mia's lie, but the more she resisted, the more I wanted to know the truth.

"But it's strange being here without my parents and my brother."

"Mia," I said, interrupting. "Did you kill someone or not?" I couldn't believe how blunt I was being.

Mia wouldn't look me in the eye. She took another swig of beer, then sat there, twisting the bottle in her hand. She stared into my newly kindled fire.

"I'm not sure," she said at last.

She wasn't sure if she'd killed someone?

"What happened?" I asked.

"My parents were gone and I was bored, so I decided to take the car out. I didn't have anywhere to be or anything, but I'd done it before, and it was dark and I figured no one would recognize me." Mia had been driving at thirteen? At first this surprised me, but Mia had done a lot of things when she was younger, including having sex with Liam. "Everything was fine—I stayed off the main roads. But side streets are really dark, and as I turned a corner, I heard these sounds. A thump. And this squeak. Metal bending. It wasn't from my car. I'd hit a guy on a bike."

"Did you stop?" I said.

"Right away. The bike was a mess, and the rider had been

thrown to one side. But the car was fine, not even any marks on the fender. I realized that if my parents found out what I'd done—that I was driving, not even that I'd hit someone—they'd never forgive me. So I got back in the car and drove off." She took a breath, held it, and let it go. "I've never told anyone that before. Anyone."

Not even Liam? I thought.

"You just left him there? Why didn't you call nine-one-one?" I tried to keep the shock out of my voice, but it didn't really work.

"Didn't have a phone."

"What makes you think he was dead?"

"I saw him. In the bushes along the road. It was dark, but he wasn't moving. Later, I overheard some people at school talking about a hit and run, about this man who'd died. I was just a dumb, scared kid, but that's no excuse. Maybe if I'd stayed, shouted for help, I could've helped him, and he wouldn't have died. I screwed up bad, and I know I'm going to pay for it after I die. I've spent the last five years trying to forget that night. I think it might be part of the reason why I am the way I am. If I'm already damned, I might as well have fun before I go, right?"

She's telling the truth. That was my very first thought. I was ninety-nine percent sure it *was* the truth. Mia had been absolutely right when she'd said that the best way to know if someone is telling the truth was to really listen.

If it *was* the truth, what did it mean? That Mia was a murderer? Or was she just another stupid kid? I honestly wasn't sure.

"Why'd you mention it last night?" I asked her. "And why are you telling me all this now?"

Outside the cabin, something clacked, like two pieces of bamboo knocking together.

Mia and I looked at each other. Either Mia had just confessed the crime of her life, or she'd tried to dump some major bullshit on me, but all that was forgotten now.

Together, we crept to the window. There weren't any shutters or drapes, but it was too dark outside to see anything anyway. Rain lashed the window, like they always say in books.

"Should we open the door?" Mia said.

"Yes," I said.

She cracked it open, and together we peered outside. Only then did it occur to me that we should go wake the others, especially Galen, but now it was too late. The torrents of rain sounded like a low-pitched groan. I suddenly became aware of how tense I was, how my shoulders were as stiff as a scarecrow's.

"See anything?" I said.

Mia shook her head.

As she did, something moved in the darkness, shooting across the yard.

"There's someone out there!" I said. I didn't even need to point, Mia had seen it too. We were both staring at the same spot now. In the light from our doorway, I could make out the pump and maybe the trunk of some trees beyond that, but that's all. A moon would have helped, but it had never risen, or maybe it was hidden behind the clouds.

The rain was coming down in buckets. If this was what it was like when the rain sounded like squirrels on the roof, how bad had it been when it sounded like deer?

"I can't believe there's anyone out in that downpour," I said. But we'd definitely seen *something*.

Without warning, Mia shouted out at the rain. "Get the hell out of here! Leave us the *fuck* alone!"

It was surprising how the water absorbed the noise. How quiet her voice sounded despite how loud she'd been.

We kept staring out as the rain washed the night. Everything was moving and nothing was moving, all at the same time.

"Water is getting in," I said. "Close the door." The rain was falling so hard it was landing on the stoop and spattering inside. A trail of silver water already oozed across the uneven floor like a snake.

Something darted across the yard again—an elk. That must've been what we'd heard before, the clatter of its hooves on the ground, and what we'd seen streak across in the dark.

That's all it was, all it had ever been. An animal.

But we didn't laugh, not like we might have earlier in the day. Everything was still way too serious.

Mia closed the door and locked it again.

We stood there a minute, and I tried to untwist the pretzel in my shoulders. I took a step forward, right into the puddle on the floor that I'd noticed only seconds before.

I felt Mia staring at me and I looked up into her eyes.

"You know, you're not who I thought you were," she said, a smile locked on her lips.

"What?"

"When I first met you. I thought you were someone different."

So it seemed that I had some mystery after all. I considered asking what kind of person she'd thought I was, but I wasn't sure I wanted to know.

"What were you going to ask me earlier?" I said.

"Huh?" she said. She scratched her tattoo.

"Before, after Galen fell asleep. You said there was something you wanted to ask me." I didn't even care if she asked me if Liam and I had been thinking about Galen while having sex. In a way, I wanted her to.

It was weird. I actually felt close to Mia now. It was like she was an actual friend, not just the best friend of my boyfriend.

It was even better than what I'd been feeling before, about finally being part of the group. As for what she'd done to that man on the bike, I didn't feel qualified to judge.

"Oh," she said. "Well, it's about Galen."

"Yeah?"

"Liam . . ."

What about him? I thought.

"Well, I know there's been some weirdness," Mia said.

So Mia had sensed it too, what was going on between Galen and Liam. It was strange how Liam was having the exact opposite reaction to this weekend that I was. I felt myself drawing closer to everyone, but he was drifting away, from Galen at least, and maybe even from Mia too. After all, Galen and Mia were boyfriend and girlfriend.

Maybe friendship is about more than tattoos, I thought. But that made me feel guilty, like I was stealing Liam's friends.

"It's fine," I said. "It'll all work out."

"It will?" Mia said.

"I promise." Liam was a really good guy, and he wasn't a child. Yeah, Galen had teased him a bit, but it hadn't been anything unforgiveable. Liam would get over it in the end, if only for Mia's sake.

She relaxed right before my eyes. It was like an actual weight had been lifted off her shoulders.

"Thanks," she said. "That really means a lot to me."

She put a hand on my arm and squeezed.

I'd surprised Mia this weekend, but she'd surprised me more. Weirdly, the fact that she'd killed someone when she was thirteen was the least of it.

"But don't tell him we talked about it, okay?" I said. "That would be weird."

She smiled and turned for the fire. "I'll keep your secret," she said over her shoulder, "if you promise to keep mine."

We didn't make pancakes the next morning. We hardly ate anything at all. Being stranded without transportation or a phone at a remote cabin with an unknown assailant lurking in the woods has a way of killing your appetite.

That's the right word, right? Assailant?

And of course it was still raining. We could hear it coming down outside, thumping squirrel-like on the roof of the cabin.

"There's no way they spent the night out here," Liam said. "Not in that rain. Not even in a car."

"They might have," Galen said, and Liam bristled a little. "All we know for sure is that they're crazy. We don't know *how* crazy. They're definitely crazy enough to follow us all the way out here and spend a whole day jerking us around, but are they also crazy enough to spend a whole *weekend*? In the rain?"

"Let's just go," Mia said. The plan was to start the long walk to the highway at first light, and it was now way past that.

I looked at the four of us, with no real rain gear whatsoever. Not a single one of us had even packed boots.

We set out on the dirt road. We'd packed a few supplies in backpacks—water, some food, some dry clothing—but left most of our stuff in the cabin. Someone would have to come back for the car anyway. As we passed the car, I could still smell the spilled gasoline—it hadn't been washed away, even in all the rain. No one said anything, but it felt strange to leave the vehicle behind. Don't they always say that if you're ever in an accident to never leave your car? But that advice obviously didn't make any sense here.

The road was muddy. *Really* muddy. So muddy that I was thirty-five percent sure we'd have gotten stuck somewhere along this road even if the car *was* running, especially on that first steep hill.

By the time we reached the top of the hill, my feet were already soaked. The mud had also somehow gotten into my socks, and the wet dirt felt like sandpaper, scraping my ankles and heels with every step.

142

Most of the mud was in the tire ruts, so we all quickly gravitated to the rocky bulge in the middle of the road. That meant walking single file. And the bulge was narrow, so it was a little like walking on a balance beam. How fast does a person normally walk? Two miles an hour? Between the mud and the rain and walking on that rocky balance beam, we were probably going half that. And how far was it to the highway? Mia had said it could be fifteen miles.

That meant it was going to be a *long* walk. That we might not even be there by nightfall.

"We don't necessarily need to walk all the way to the main road," Mia said. "We only need to walk far enough that there's a signal." She meant for our cell phones, and that reminded her to check hers right then, shielding it from the rain with her hand. But there wasn't a signal, just like I knew there wouldn't be. In fact, there was no guarantee there was going to be a signal even out on the highway. But if we did make it to the main road, we could at least flag down a passing car.

Before long, the rain forest fell away, and the muddy road stretched out into a clear-cut. Little streams washed down over the landscape, all of the water brown with dirt. The runoff cut trenches in the road itself, sometimes even through the bulge in the middle.

In a way, the clear-cut was kind of a relief. If it really was the Brummits stalking us, who's to say they weren't hiding in the lush rain forest, watching us? We knew for a fact the family had a crossbow, probably more than one, and lots of guns too. But here in the clear-cut, the piles of stripped branches had mostly rotted away, and the seedlings barely came up past our ankles, so there was no place for anyone to hide.

We slogged forward, stepping over little canyons in the road. No one said anything, but I kept thinking how stupid it was, the whole idea of chopping a forest up into parcels. It was like trying to slice a balloon—impossible. It was all or nothing. Or maybe it was like a person: you couldn't cut someone up into pieces and expect him to live.

We'd only been walking fifteen minutes, and we were already drenched. My feet were blistering from the mud.

At the head of the line, Galen stopped. We all stopped behind him.

"What is it?" Mia said.

Up ahead of us, the clear-cut ended and the forest started again. In the rain, the trees looked like a big black wall. There was another cave-like opening where the road disappeared into the rain forest, and somehow this was even blacker than everything else.

Galen took it all in. He fiddled with the strings on his hoodie.

"This is a mistake," he said at last.

"What?" Liam said.

Galen turned to us. "Don't you see? This is what they *want* us to do. Why they sabotaged our car. They knew we'd walk out along this road."

"What are you saying?" Mia said.

"I'm saying this was a bad idea! Walking to the highway!" Galen was angry, jittery, a bundle of nerves. It was way more than his usual afternoon crankiness.

"We can't stay at the cabin," Mia said.

"Why not?"

"You know why not," she said. It was funny how the sound

of the falling rain made everyone speak louder. Not quite shouting, but like we were standing next to a roaring train.

"Think about it," Galen said. "If you don't show up later tonight, your parents are going to call you. When they can't reach you on your phone, they're going to call the cops. Then they'll send someone out to check on us, the sheriff or someone. Your parents know exactly where we are. The only reason you wouldn't answer your phone is if something had happened. If you couldn't get back to the road somehow."

Mia thought for a second, then said, "You're right!" She sounded incredibly relieved, like she'd just defused a bomb with three seconds to go. She turned to Liam and me. "He's right! All we have to do is wait in the cabin and everything will be fine. Fuck, I bet the sheriff'll be here before midnight!"

"And if the cops don't come, your parents will," Galen said. "It's only a three-hour drive."

I realized I'd somehow stepped off the bulge in the middle of the road and into the mud. As we stood there, I could actually feel myself sinking deeper, like it was quicksand. I knew I should move, but part of me didn't want to, that I'd discover I was already in too deep.

"So . . . what?" Liam said. "We go back to the cabin and wait?"

Galen turned back to the rain forest, the mud squelching under his feet. He didn't answer, just stared into the black hole in front of us. He twisted the strings on his hoodie again.

"You really think they could be waiting for us in there?" Mia asked.

"Do *you* wanna chance it?" Galen said.

Mia, Liam, and I all looked at one another. When the options are all bad, it's hard to decide which one is best.

"I think Galen's right," Mia said. "My parents aren't going to leave us out here. And we were fine in the cabin all night long."

Mia and Galen were in agreement, but were Liam and I? I looked at him, asking him the question with my eyes. This wasn't like the day before, when I'd really wanted to leave. This time I honestly didn't know what we should do.

The rain thrummed down, and Liam shuffled his feet—he looked as uncertain as I felt.

"That's it then," Galen said.

He turned and started back for the cabin. Mia followed right behind him.

If you'd asked me before that weekend, I would've said that Mia was the leader of our little group, and in a lot of ways, she was. But when push came to shove, it was Galen who was in charge.

Glumly, Liam and I turned and followed too.

For a long time, the only sound was our feet sloshing in the mud.

Finally, Mia said, "Hey! Maybe someone will see us on Google Earth. You can zoom in, right? Maybe our parents are looking down at us right now. They know exactly where we are." Mia looked up at the sky and started waving her arms. "Help!" she shouted.

I honestly wasn't sure if she was serious or not.

"Google Earth isn't live," Liam said.

She glanced back at him. "It isn't?"

He shook his head. "They update it every two weeks. But even then it's not usually new data, especially not in places like this."

She looked back up at the sky and started waving her arms again. "Never mind!"

We all smiled, relaxing a bit at last.

As for me, I couldn't help wondering where we'd be two weeks from now, when the satellite images of us might finally be live. In one sense, we'd still be here on this muddy road, cold and wet, with Mia waving her hands up at the clouds. But where would we be for real?

I hoped we'd be home and safe, this whole weird weekend long forgotten. But for the first time, I was seriously starting to wonder if we would.

The one good thing about all the mud was that it meant everyone left footprints, at least until the rain eventually washed them away. When we got back to the cabin, I searched the mud and moss, and saw what looked to be the same footprints we'd left behind: Mia's Nike slip-ons, Galen's hipster moccasins, Liam's Keds. So unless they could levitate, we knew for a fact no one had been there while we were gone.

We rinsed our shoes and socks in the basin by the pump, but the mud had soaked in deep. They didn't get very clean. Once inside the cabin, we left our shoes by the door and put the socks up by the fireplace to dry, even though the fire had long since burned out.

"I have an idea," Galen announced.

Of course you do, I thought. I glanced at Liam, and he rolled his eyes.

"We can set up an early warning system," Galen said. "Some kind of alarm."

"Alarm?" Mia said. "With no electricity and no supplies?"

"Let me see what I can come up with," he said. He started going through the drawers and cupboards.

Liam moved toward the door.

"Where are you going?" Mia asked.

"If we're staying here, we're going to need more firewood," he said.

"I don't think any of us should be alone right now," Galen said.

Without hesitating, I nodded and turned for my shoes. But Liam didn't wait. He'd left the cabin in his bare feet.

In the end, I followed Liam out into the yard in my bare feet too. The moss was cool and much wetter than I expected, like walking on soggy paper towels. It actually felt good after all the gritty mud rubbing in my shoes and socks.

The rain had stopped, which sort of figured. The trees still dripped—more than before because of the rain. But for all that water, the world didn't smell clean. The air smelled sour, like something rotten. All the rain must have stirred up the nearby bog.

I stared out into the undergrowth beyond the yard. I shivered. It gave me the creeps, knowing there was someone out there, maybe even watching me right now.

I looked down at the lake and noticed a heron standing motionless in the reeds, waiting for a fish or frog to swim by. A mist rose up from the surface of the lake, like a pot right before the water begins to boil. I glanced back at the heron in the reeds, but now I saw I was wrong: there was no heron, and there never had been. It was just a clump of sticks. I'd seen something out of the corner of my eye and my brain had filled in the details. It was the opposite of that island Mia had showed me the day before. That had been right in front of my face all along and I hadn't been able to see it. Now here was this heron I thought I'd seen, but it hadn't really ever been there at all.

I found Liam squatting down, picking through the scraps

of wood in the firewood shed along the side of the cabin. Staying up all night in shifts, we had long since burned the wood we'd brought with us, and it had been years since Mia and her family had been up to the cabin, so whatever scraps of wood had been left in the shed had mostly rotted in the damp rain forest air.

"You okay?" I said.

He turned to look up at me. "What?"

"I know it's bugging you that Galen took charge."

Liam shrugged. "Whatever. I get it. Straight guys need to feel like they're in control. That's not what's bugging me."

"Then what?" I asked.

Liam hesitated. Our voices weren't echoing off the lake anymore, not the way they had yesterday. Did it have something to do with the mist?

"Something about this whole thing doesn't add up," he said at last. "I mean, take the satellite phone. Someone steals our phone, but we realize it's missing, so they put it back. Then they steal it again the next day? How is that even possible? Wouldn't someone have *seen* them?"

I nodded, even as I shivered again. Now it was from the cold. I'd left my jacket inside, and the chill of the water on my feet was making my whole body shake.

"But that's what happened," I said. "Either that, or we really did misplace the phone the night before, and then they stole it for real."

"I know, I know," Liam said. "But that doesn't feel right. I mean, it sounds preposterous."

I didn't say anything for a second, just scratched my wrist. Then I nodded to the shed and said, "There's no wood, is there?"

"Nothing usable. And there's no point looking out there," he said, meaning the nearby trees. "Everything is so damn wet. I feel like I'm never going to be dry again."

I stared out at the dripping rain forest. If I hadn't known better, I would've sworn it was closer now, that it was inching in on us.

He stood up and stepped closer to me. I immediately took him in my arms. I know a lot of girls like guys to be bigger than they are so they can feel protected, and a lot of guys like girls to be smaller so they can feel like protectors. But one of the things I loved about being with Liam, about being with a guy, is that we were the same size. It felt more like a relationship between equals, not just emotionally, but physically too. Two halves of one whole.

"We're going to get through this," I said. "Two weeks from now, when Google Earth is finally getting around to showing us hugging next to this firewood shed, you and I are going to be home and content. And *dry*. Really, really dry."

I expected Liam to laugh or at least say something, but he was looking intently down at the ground. He pulled away and bent over, digging for something in the moss.

"What is it?" I said.

He picked something up with his left hand and held it out to me. "It's a match," he said. It hadn't been lit.

"So?"

He looked over at the barrel where the fire had burned the day before, only five or six feet away.

"Liam?" I said. "What is it?"

He ignored me and stepped closer to the barrel. He leaned down to look inside, at the ashes of yesterday's fire.

"Liam?"

He turned around and showed me the match again. "This is how they lit the fire. A match like this. If it was an old match, it'd be rotten."

"I guess. So what?"

"So whoever lit that fire yesterday must've dropped it by accident."

"Okay," I said. "Again, so what? Are you planning on dusting it for fingerprints?"

"No, but look at it." He held it up to me one more time.

I still had no idea what he was getting at.

"It's *blue*," he said. "The head."

"So?"

"So most matches are red."

"And?"

"The matches in the box we brought with us are blue!"

I remembered the matches we'd been using all weekend. They were still on the mantle by the fireplace. And they were definitely blue. But I didn't see what Liam was getting at.

"Don't you see?" he said. "One of *us* lit that fire."

I tried to understand what he was saying, but it still didn't make any sense. "Just because it was lit with matches from inside the cabin? But the cabin was unlocked. It's *always* unlocked."

Liam started pacing back and forth, his bare feet squishing in the soggy moss.

"It never really made sense." Liam was thinking out loud. "Not just the satellite phone. All of it. So what if the Brummits are angry with Mia's parents and grandparents? Mia's family *knows* they're angry. I bet the whole county knows they're angry. I can't believe they'd be stupid enough to pick an open fight like this. People out here must sell land to logging companies all the time. So who's going to take the Brummits' side on this? And even if they *are* pissed off enough to risk being arrested, are they really going to lurk around pulling pranks in the rain for forty-eight hours? If they're that angry, and that crazy, why not light the cabin on fire and be done with it? Why didn't they set this cabin on fire years ago?"

"Because it wouldn't burn in the rain forest, for one thing," I said.

"Rob, you're missing the point."

"Besides, I'm not saying it was the adults. I'm saying it was their kids."

"Because of something that happened three years ago? Because someone did something to their parents' cabin's *view*? Does that sound like something their kids would care about? No. Let's face it. The whole thing with the Brummits, we were totally jumping to conclusions."

We weren't totally jumping to conclusions—*I* was. It had been my theory from the start. But I guess I could see what Liam was getting at.

"So it isn't the Brummits," I said. "So it's some backwoods loner. Or some kids on mountain bikes."

"There weren't any other tire tracks on the road coming in. And there haven't been any other footprints around the cabin either, even in all the moss and mud. Just ours. If this is a bunch of kids, they must be part elf."

"But someone *was* here," I said. "Someone lit that fire. And someone stole our phone and poked holes in the gas tank of the car."

"Don't you *get* it?" he said, almost angry. "It was one of *us*. All of it. The fire, the outhouse, the car. As for the phone, who else could have taken it twice, right out from under our noses?"

"But why would one of *us* have done all those things? I mean, strand us here without a phone or a car? That goes way beyond any prank."

"How well do we know Galen anyway?"

I laughed, but Liam didn't.

"Wait . . . ," I said. "You're serious?"

"Think it through. He was the one who suggested we come to this cabin in the first place. And he was the one who said we should come back to the cabin today, that we shouldn't try to walk out to the main road. He was also the one who didn't want to leave yesterday. And what's with the mood swings? One minute he's all cool and hipster, the next minute he's jumpy and irritated. He's *nervous* about something."

I was pretty sure this was really about the fact that Liam didn't like Galen.

"Let's just slow down," I said, trying to sound patient.

Liam shook his head. "No! This is the only thing that makes any sense. Galen also knew exactly how to sabotage the car. No one else knew where to poke the holes. And he was the one who suggested we check to see if it was still running."

"He did that for me, because I was upset," I said. "And he's not nervous. He just gets moody in the afternoon. You know that. And how does it make sense that he was able to light a fire from miles away? Galen was with the rest of us up on that hill when that fire started burning."

"He delayed it somehow," Liam said. He turned back toward the metal barrel and leaned down inside, rooting around in the ashes themselves. "He set everything up, then used some kind of time-delayed fuse to actually light the fire." He voice echoed in the barrel. "A slow-burning wood or a stick of incense." He bolted upright, a small wad of melted wax in his hand. "A candle! He lit a taper in the bin, but it didn't burn down to reach the paper and the kindling until we were almost up the hill!"

I hesitated. I'd thought the blue match was just a coincidence, but the melted wax? It did sort of fit what Liam was saying.

Then I remembered. "Mia said they use that bin to burn garbage. So they once burned something made of wax." Before Liam could object, I added, "Besides, we still don't have a why. *Why* would Galen do all this?"

"Because he likes jerking people around! Think it *through*. You saw the way he acted when we were skinny-dipping. What was all that about? And going skinny-dipping was *his* idea!" Liam twitched he was so angry.

He had another good point. Galen had definitely known what he was doing that night at the lake. He clearly liked screwing with people, and he also liked being in control. He was mechanically minded, the kind of person who invented watering guns and makeshift alarm systems, exactly the kind of person to rig up something like the candle in the fire bin. And while it had been my idea to go away in the first place, it was Galen who'd come up with the idea of coming to this cabin. What had he said? That he'd seen a photo of it at Mia's house? I'd been to Mia's house—only once, but still—and I didn't remember any photo.

Then there was our game of Three Truths and Lie. Galen

had been the best liar by far, the only one who'd fooled everyone, at least without cheating like Mia.

I didn't tell Liam what I was thinking because I didn't want to encourage him. What if we were wrong? But I was starting to think there was at least a forty percent chance we weren't.

"It's Galen," Liam was saying. "It's Occam's razor."

"What?" I said.

"That's the principle that says the simplest explanation for something is usually the right one. If you think you hear horses, it's probably horses, not zebras."

"You think the simplest explanation for all this is that the longtime boyfriend of your best friend joined us at a cabin in the rain forest so he could secretly harass us? That Mia just happens to be dating a serial killer?"

Liam stopped twitching. He stopped moving entirely. "Who said anything about a serial killer?" he said.

"I didn't mean he's a *serial killer*," I said quickly. "I just meant that the whole thing is crazy."

"Seriously, Rob! Who said anything about a serial killer? You really think we're in that much danger?" For all his amazing brain power, Liam's confidence could be squashed like a bug.

"No," I said as firmly as I knew how. "Not at all." I stepped forward and hugged him again, even if he now felt stiff and tense in my arms, even if my bare feet were colder than ever in the wet moss.

As I held him, he asked in a muffled voice, "So what do we do now?"

But my own bravado had been all an act. I didn't have the slightest clue what to do next.

"Maybe we can get Galen to admit what he's done," I said.

Liam nodded, but at that point, I wasn't sure I even wanted to know the truth.

When Liam and I rounded the corner back to the front of the cabin, Mia was stringing something throughout the yard.

"What's going on?" I asked.

"Oh, hey," she said. "Look what we found." She held up a roll of fishing line. She'd already wound the line all around the area in front of the cabin: out to the water pump, over to the car, even all the way to the closest trees of the rain forest. It was all about a foot off the ground, and looked a little like a big flat spider's web.

"But what . . ."

She tugged on one of the lines. Something rattled—metal pots?—in a clump of ferns near the front door. "It's Galen's alarm system. Anyone trips over the line, and we know he's out here. Pretty clever, huh?"

I looked around the yard, at how the line crisscrossed everywhere. It was fishing line, designed to be invisible to fish, but it wasn't really invisible, not out of the water and not in the daylight. The lines were like tiny blue lasers.

"What do you think?" Mia asked us.

"I don't know," I said. "I can see it all."

"It'll work better in the dark."

When Mia pushed open the front door, Galen said, "Stop! Wait! Go slow."

He was standing just inside the door, duct-taping three empty tin cans to the back of the door itself.

"What's this?" I asked as Liam, Mia, and I squeezed our way past him. I could smell his sweat and, annoyingly, it smelled good.

"The cans are full of nails," Galen said. "If anyone opens the door, they'll rattle." He tested the setup a few times, opening and closing the door. Sure enough, the nails rattled at least a little, no matter how carefully he tried to open the door.

I stared at Galen, who was totally immersed in his

contraption. He almost looked happy to be working on such a clear puzzle to be solved. But this was no game. It was our warning against a crazy person who was trying to scare the hell out of us, or worse. Did Galen look the way he did because that's the way he was, or was it because the crazy person was him and he knew he didn't have anything to worry about? I thought about all the things that had happened: the outhouse, the fire, the car, the satellite phone. Had Galen had the opportunity to slip away and do all those things unnoticed? I hadn't been paying attention to him, so I didn't know.

"Whaddaya think?" Galen said.

"I guess it'll work," I said.

"So a nail walks into a bar and says to the bartender, 'I really need to get hammered!'" Galen said.

Clearly he was perking back up, becoming his usual mellow self, but I wondered how even he could make jokes at a time like this.

Before anyone could respond, Liam said, "There's no more firewood."

"We'll have to burn the coffee table," Galen said. "And the chairs and tables if it comes to that."

Galen had collected a bunch of stuff on the dinner table: a hammer and more nails, a wad of rubber bands, at least ten old-fashioned mousetraps, wire and string, a faded box of rat poison, aluminum foil, and even that box of blue-tipped matches from the fireplace mantle.

"This is all the stuff we have?" I said.

He looked over. "All the stuff that seemed like it might help us."

I looked back at the nails on the table, and remembered what Galen had said about how someone had punctured our gas tank with either a screwdriver or a nail. But if he'd done it, why would he have told us what he did it with?

"I was thinking," Galen said, "that we could put mouse-traps outside under the windows, and inside on the window-sills too. They make a lot of noise when they go off. And once they're set, they go off even if you barely touch 'em."

"We're probably going to be here for at least eight more hours," Mia said. "What we really need is a gun."

A *gun*? The word was like a hiccup in time. For some reason, just the sound of it seemed to change things. Fishing line alarms and mousetraps were one thing, but what were we going to do with a gun? Shoot someone?

"A gun is *exactly* what we need," Galen said. He looked at Mia. "Your parents don't keep one here, do they?"

She shook her head. "They don't even keep sharp knives in the kitchen."

"They say a dull knife is actually more dangerous than a sharp one," I said.

"Not if you're using it as a weapon," Galen said matter-of-factly.

"Wait a minute," Mia said. "My parents don't keep a gun in our cabin, but maybe the Brummits do."

We all stared at her. Time hiccupped again. Or maybe it was more than a hiccup. Somehow I knew that what Mia had just said had somehow altered the course of our weekend. For better or for worse, whatever happened from now on was going to be different than if she'd never said those words.

Given that we were talking about a gun, it was probably for the worse.

"Really?" Galen said. "You think they might have a gun?" Of course he was excited.

"Well, I can't be sure," Mia said. "But they *are* hunters."

Unlike Mia's parents, they keep their cabin locked up, I thought. Maybe that meant they had something worth locking.

"Wait," Liam said. "We're worried about being harassed by the Brummits, so we're going to go break into their cabin and steal their gun?"

"Why not?" Galen said. "They're not there. Or at least they weren't yesterday. If they're back there now, then we can have this out with them once and for all. And if they're not, we can see if they have any weapons we can use. I bet it never occurred to them we'd do *that*."

"Hold on," Liam said. "This is crazy. We can't go all the way over there again just because they *might* have a gun. And we can't break into their cabin! If they're mad now, think how pissed they'd be then."

"They're *already* pissed," Mia said. "Look at all the things they've done. And if we *do* find a gun, maybe we can finally fight back."

"None of us even knows how to use a gun," I said.

"I do," Galen said, which also figured. "Besides, it's not just a gun we might find over there. Maybe they have a satellite phone or something else we could use."

"Still," Liam said, "we're finally getting the cabin protected. Now we're going to leave it again?"

Galen looked at Mia. "He's got a point about that. Some-one should probably stay here. Why don't you and I go to the Brummits?"

"But that's *crazy*!" Liam said. "There's someone *out* there! You don't know what they're capable of!" He was twitching again, but not out of anger. Now it was fear. I'm not sure I'd ever seen his eyes open so wide.

But I was confused. Liam *didn't* think there was someone out there, the Brummits or anyone. He thought Galen was behind the pranks.

He's worried about Mia, I realized. He thought Galen was going to do something to her if the two of them went off alone.

"I think our splitting up is a really bad idea," I said. If Liam supported me, the least I could do was support him.

"We'll be fine," Galen said in his usual don't-question-me way.

"Mia, please!" Liam said. "I really don't think this is a good idea."

"Liam," Mia said, "you're worrying too much. It'll be fine."

"Then let's all go!" Liam said.

"No, no," Galen said. "You had a really good point. We're finally getting our alarm system set up. I don't want those assholes coming in and disabling everything, or setting some trap for us. Mia and I'll run over and see if there's a gun or a phone. If there is, our problems are pretty much solved. If there's not, we'll come back and finish what we started here. Either way, we'll be back in fifteen minutes, tops."

"But—"

"Liam, relax," Mia said. "Nothing's going to happen."

After they left, Liam paced frantically back and forth across the cabin. Galen had suggested that we get started with the mousetraps, but the two of us didn't have the slightest clue how to set a mousetrap. Besides, Liam was way too distracted.

"How long has it been?" he asked.

"About two minutes," I said.

"I can't believe this! That was obviously all an excuse for him to get Mia alone."

"But it was Mia's idea."

Liam stared at me like I was an idiot. "He *wanted* her to suggest it. That's why he suggested this stupid alarm system in the first place. He's manipulating us. *Her*."

Was this true? Was anyone really that smart?

"I think we should follow them," he said.

"But Galen said to stay here," I said.

He gave me a look like a boxer's punch. "*Really?* We should listen to the guy who's been jerking us around all weekend? The guy I'm worried is going to hurt my best friend?"

So this was what it came down to: did I ultimately believe Liam or not? Was Galen really the guy behind everything that had happened this weekend or was it someone else?

At this point, I was seventy percent sure Liam was right, that Galen was behind it, so I said, "Okay, let's go."

We put our socks and shoes back on. Outside, we listened for a moment, but didn't hear anything. Mia and Galen were gone, but they'd left fresh tracks in the moss and mud. We followed them to the dirt road, then down toward the cabin at the other end of the lake. Only then did it occur to me that we should've brought some kind of weapon—the poker from the fireplace or a knife from the kitchen, even a dull one. But it seemed too late now so I didn't say anything.

As usual, the trees dripped. We quickly came to the bog again, where the road got even muddier. Galen and Mia's footprints disappeared. They must have started walking on the grassy bulge in the middle of the road.

Over in the lake, something splashed. Loudly.

"What was that?" Liam whispered.

"An animal?" I said.

We'd been hearing birds and fish splashing in the lake all weekend, but this sounded like something else, something bigger. Maybe it was an elk or a moose. As Liam and I stared over at the water, we saw something we hadn't seen the day before: a narrow trail that meandered toward the lake. It skirted the edges of the swamp, avoiding any actual pools.

I knew Liam was thinking that Mia and Galen might have taken this trail, that maybe they were the ones who'd made the splash. There were no footprints here either, but the trail was mostly rotten leaves so maybe there wouldn't *be* any footprints.

"Should we check it out?" I said.

"I guess," he said.

I led the way down the trail. It was only a few yards before the lake came more into sight. I couldn't see what had made the splash—there was still too much undergrowth—but I did see faint ripples rolling out from shore.

I pushed onward, working my way through the alders. Part of me wondered if this was even a trail at all, or just random patches of bare ground. So far things on Moon Lake had a way of never being exactly what they seemed.

Before I knew it, I found myself in the middle of a thick patch of devil's walkingstick.

"Rob!" Liam whispered behind me. "I heard something!"

I turned back toward him. He'd been lucky enough to stop outside the patch of thorns.

"Over by the cabin!" He stared at me, eyes wide again.

"Well, let's go," I said.

But as I started back toward the main road, my sleeve

174

caught in the thorns. The more I struggled, the more caught up I became. Water still dripped down from above, getting all over my glasses. It was hard to make out anything through the droplets on my lenses, but I did see Liam disappearing through the undergrowth.

"Liam!" I said, but he didn't stop.

I finally got myself free of that one plant, but I still wasn't out of the briar. I inched forward, carefully pushing the thorny stalks away from me so they wouldn't catch on my clothes. But the plants were thick and interconnected, and the more I pushed, the more other branches reached out to snag me. It was weird how much easier it had been to get into this situation than it was to get out again.

Eventually I was free, but by then Liam was long gone.

I hurried back to the main road. Once there, I turned right, toward the Brummits' cabin. Liam hadn't left any footprints in the mud either.

Someone gasped. It sounded perfectly clear, though I was still too far from the cabin to see anything. Mia had said animals could make surprisingly humanlike sounds. Is that what this was?

I ran down the road, careful to avoid slipping into the mud.

"Help!" Liam called. *"Help!"*

My blood flash-froze. These weren't animal sounds! For an instant, even the trees seemed to stop their dripping. Time hadn't just slowed, it had stopped completely.

Then I ran forward even faster than before. Now I didn't care about the mud.

The land rose up, and the cabin came into sight. But I didn't see anyone around, not Liam, and not Galen or Mia. The deflated inflatable stuck in the crook of the tree caught my eye—pink and yellow, but old and covered in grime.

Mia screamed.

I followed the sound of her scream to the far side of the cabin, near the outhouse. Mia and Liam both stood there, frozen, staring down. Time had stopped again.

Galen lay on the ground in front of them. He was stretched out, facedown on his stomach.

Like he was dead.

Why did I think Galen was dead? It was something about the position of his body. It wasn't that he'd fallen forward. It was more like he'd collapsed where he stood, and then toppled forward. Galen had the body of a natural athlete, but now his leg was bent and his arms were twisted helplessly at his sides, like he hadn't even tried to catch himself.

Galen can't be dead, I thought. *Can he?*

I ran toward them. Halfway there I saw the wound on Galen's head. It was on the left side in back, about the size of a quarter, dark, almost black. His hair was matted like it was wet, but with blood, not water.

Liam crouched down next to the gawky heap of Galen's body, examining it, hands out, but not daring to touch it.

"What happened?" I said. I could barely get the words out.

"I don't know, I don't know!" Mia said, panicking. "*Do something!*"

I squatted down next to Liam, but I couldn't bring myself to touch the body either. This was beyond any first aid I'd ever been taught. Even so, I forced myself to roll him over.

He was so limp. It wasn't like the bodies of dead people on television, clearly just actors pretending. I'd never seen anything like this before.

His eyes were open, but they weren't looking anywhere. They might as well have been marbles. His mouth was open too, but there was something wrong with his tongue. It already looked swollen.

"Is he okay?" Mia said. "Is he going to be okay?"

I didn't know how to answer. I also didn't know what to do. Should we bandage his head, to try to stop the bleeding? Liam was already stripping off his sweatshirt and pressing it against the wound in the back of Galen's head.

I knew how to do mouth-to-mouth. Should I do it? Galen wasn't breathing, that much was obvious.

I pushed his tongue down, deeper into his mouth. His

tongue felt weird, stiff, but it was definitely still warm. So I tipped his head, plugged his nose, and started blowing into him.

Galen's body didn't just look limp, it *felt* limp. The skin itself, his lips against mine, everything sagged. He was like a balloon I couldn't fill up. He didn't feel anything like the dummy I'd learned mouth-to-mouth on, except that neither one felt like it was alive.

I stopped blowing and felt his neck for a pulse. When he'd been on his stomach, the blood from his head wound had dripped down around the front of his neck, so I could feel it, sticky and already cold. I didn't feel anything beating under all that blood.

"Is he okay?" Mia said. "Is he going to be okay?"

I didn't answer. Instead, I started doing CPR. Galen was wearing a jacket, which I opened, and a T-shirt, which I yanked up. I measured and positioned the heels of my palms, like they'd taught us in first aid. His chest looked so different than when we'd gone skinny-dipping. His skin was still gold, but now the luster was gone.

I started pushing. "One and two and three and four," I counted out loud.

Immediately call for help. This was something else I remembered from first aid. The most important part of CPR was to immediately have someone call nine-one-one or go for help. That was the whole *point* of first aid—to try to keep the person alive until real medical help arrived.

But there was no way to call nine-one-one from here. There was no way to call anyone for help. Even by car, we were over an hour from the nearest road, and our car was out of gas.

How long should I keep doing CPR? In first aid, they said to keep doing it until help arrives, as long as it takes. Because if they're still not breathing, if their heart isn't pumping, and you stop, then the person really will die.

Except that Galen was already dead. I wasn't qualified to say that, but I still knew it to be true. I could tell just by touch. This thing that had happened here was no mere prank.

I stopped and sat back on my heels.

"What are you doing?" Mia said. "Don't stop! Don't fucking *stop!*"

I looked up at her, but I didn't say anything. There was nothing I could say.

"No," she said. Dry heaves rose up from her gut. "No!"

Liam stood and put his arms around her, comforting her. She let herself *be* comforted, which surprised me a little. The water in the trees dripped down from above. In books, they always say stuff like this feels like some kind of baptism, but the truth was it felt more like we were being pissed on.

"What happened here?" I said. Had Mia killed Galen? Liam had been worried that Galen might do something bad to Mia. Had he been right, but she'd fought him off and killed him in the process?

When she didn't answer, I repeated, "Mia? Who did this?"

"I don't know," Mia said, her voice hollow.

I looked at Liam, but he didn't know either. I glanced around for the weapon, but there was nothing I could see, no ski poles or croquet mallets lying in the moss.

"How could you not know?" I said to Mia. "Weren't you and Galen together?"

"No," she said. She stiffened, and her eyes found their

focus on the trees around us. "We need to get back to our cabin. Whoever did this is still out here."

Mia was saying she hadn't done this, and I was somehow seventy-five percent sure she was telling the truth. Which meant Liam had been wrong: there *was* someone stalking us after all. Was it the Brummits? Had *they* killed Galen? But where had they gone? If they'd done this, they had to still be nearby. Maybe they were planning on killing us too. Maybe they already had us in their crossbow sights.

"Come *on*," Mia said. "We need to *go*."

I jerked into motion, but now I felt Mia's eyes on me. Somehow I knew that when she'd said "we," she meant Galen too. So I slung him over my shoulders and lifted him. I'd expected him to be heavy, but still didn't expect the body to be so limp, so obviously dead. His pants were wet, and at first I thought it was water from the ground, but then I smelled what it really was: he'd pissed himself. But it's not like I could say anything about it.

The farther I carried the body, the heavier it seemed to be. I staggered under the weight of it. Something hard in the breast of his jacket pressed into my back—his phone or his wallet. As we approached the bog, I saw the muddy pools in the road again. I tried stepping up onto the bulge in the middle of the road, but with Galen on my back, it was too narrow and I kept losing my balance. Finally, I just stepped back into the water, which splashed under my feet. It was cold and slimy, but I went slowly so I didn't slip.

All the way, I kept expecting to hear a shot or a snap from the trees around me, to feel a bullet or an arrow piercing me, but nothing ever did.

We made it back to the clearing around the cabin at last. With the weight on my shoulders, I had a hard time stepping over the fishing line Mia had stretched all over the yard. It was a good defense against people carrying dead bodies at least.

Once inside, I carried Galen back into the bedroom and laid him out on the bed. I arranged the body as respectably as I could, and I closed his eyes. Then I returned to the front room, softly closing the bedroom door behind me.

I crossed to the front door to make sure it was locked, both the lock in the knob and also the dead bolt. Then I turned to

Mia, who was kneeling in front of the fireplace lighting a fire. She or Liam had broken up one of the kitchen chairs for wood.

"What happened over there?" I asked her.

She didn't answer right away, and I didn't ask again. I stepped closer, watching while the wood in the fireplace caught. Then Mia jammed it with the iron poker until it flamed brightly. In spite of everything, I was glad for that fire, for a chance to keep the Big Bad Wolf away.

Finally Mia peeled off her jacket and sat down in one of the chairs. It was only then that I realized how muddy my shoes were, how I wished I'd taken them off before coming back into the house, even with Galen on my shoulders. I'd left tracks everywhere. But it was too late to do anything about it now.

"I broke into the cabin," Mia said at last. The quiver in her voice was totally out of character. "I was looking for a gun, just like we said. I thought Galen was with me, but the next thing I knew, he was gone. Then I heard something outside"—she looked at Liam—"you calling for help. I went out, and found you. And Galen was dead. It all happened so fast. What did *you* see?"

I looked over at Liam now too, sitting in the chair opposite her.

"Well," he said, "I was on the way to the cabin, and I heard
a noise. A thud, almost a crack. It was perfectly clear through
the trees. It came from the direction of the cabin, so I ran. I
found Galen laying facedown on the ground. I was confused.
The way he looked, the fact that he was there at all—it didn't
make any sense. I started calling for help, and a second later"—
he looked at Mia—"you joined me."

So Mia had gone into the cabin, and somehow Galen
had disappeared, gone outside. Someone had come up
behind him and hit him on the head, hard enough to break
his skull, at least that's what it looked like. Liam had heard
the sound through the trees and run to investigate, but by
the time he got there, the killer was gone. That must have
been Liam's gasp I'd heard, when he'd seen Galen's dead
body. Then Liam had shouted for help, and Mia had heard
him and gone outside.

Something was wrong. It was like what Liam had said
before: the story didn't add up. Why had Liam heard the

sound, but Mia hadn't? She was inside, true, but she was also a lot closer.

"We can't just stay here," Mia said, now more agitated than upset. "We need to *do* something. We need to go." In her nervousness, she returned to the fire and prodded it with the poker. The flames erupted again.

That's when I realized she was poking it with her left hand.

Mia was left-handed?

The wound on Galen's head had been on the left side. Exactly where it would be if he'd been hit from behind by someone left-handed.

Mia had killed Galen? Her version of events was a lie?

But why would she do it? Because he'd attacked her first? Or maybe she'd realized he was the one terrorizing us and somehow lost her temper. But either way, why wouldn't she just tell us? Why make up the story about how Galen had suddenly slipped away from her?

Unless . . .

Unless she was the one doing everything in the first place. Why had Liam assumed it was Galen anyway? Because he was mechanical and liked to tease gay guys? What kind of evidence was that?

And Mia had *already* killed someone. Or at least let someone die. She said she'd been upset about it, but she hadn't been so upset that she'd done anything, not even make an anonymous phone call when she got home. And that was when she was thirteen years old.

But still, why would she do it? Not killing Galen—I could imagine a couple of different reasons for that. Why would she spend this whole weekend tormenting Liam and me? Liam was her best friend, and I was his boyfriend. *She* got the two of us together. She really seemed to care about Liam, and she liked me too, unless our conversation the night before had all been a complete lie.

A complete lie?

Mia loved lies. She'd said as much during Three Truths and a Lie. And the more complicated the lie, the more devious the teller was, the more she liked it. Maybe even her story about her killing the biker had been a lie. Not as part of any party game, but a bigger lie, one that sounded true, so I'd ask her about it later and she could stoically confess to everything and make me think we were bonding. It was a lie within a lie within a lie. Maybe this whole weekend was nothing but a game of lies, and I'd been a big, gullible idiot to fall for it all.

"How?" I said, questioning Mia's sudden desire to leave. "We still have no way out. There's no car, and it's too far to walk. The whole point was to wait here until your parents realize you're not home and call the cops." I turned on my phone and checked the clock. "That should only be about seven hours now." But even as I was saying this, I wondered if staying here was still the best idea. If Mia had killed Galen and done all those other things, did we want to stay in this cabin with her? On the other hand, if we started for the highway with her, maybe she'd lead us off track, deeper into the woods—somewhere her parents didn't know about, where the sheriff would never find us. It was a maze back here, and Liam and I didn't know these old logging roads at all. We'd have to go along with whatever Mia told us, even if it meant her leading us somewhere where she could torment us in peace.

"I can't believe he's dead," Mia said. She'd sunk down to the floor in front of the fire, awkwardly clutching the shaft of the poker even though it was probably covered with soot. She was back to being in shock. If she had killed Galen, she was a good actor, I had to give her that.

What if she didn't mean to do anything to Liam and me at all? What if this whole weekend had been all about Galen? About something in their relationship, something I didn't know anything about? In that case, the horrible part was over.

"I need to be with him," Mia said. She stood. There was soot all over her hands, but I wasn't one to talk, not with all the mud on my shoes.

"Go," Liam said comfortingly. "Take your time."

She nodded somberly. Then she walked to the bedroom door so tenderly that her feet didn't even make a creak on the floor. She closed the door behind her just as quietly.

I immediately turned to Liam. "It was Mia!" I whispered. "I think she killed Galen!"

"What?" he said. "What are you talking about?"

"It wasn't Galen. It never was. All along, I think it's been Mia. The fire, the satellite phone, the car. She was the one who 'misplaced' the phone in the first place, and the one who conveniently found it again the next day."

"Rob," Liam said, "this is crazy. It wasn't Mia."

"How do you know?"

"Are you kidding? Didn't you see how broken up she was? You think that was an act?"

"Maybe!" I said. "She's left-handed." I explained about the wound on Galen's head.

"You've been watching too many detective shows. It's probably not even true that if someone left-handed attacks someone else, they leave an injury on that side of their body. It probably totally depends."

"But her story doesn't make sense," I said. I remembered how thin the walls to the bedroom were, and I lowered my voice even softer. "She said she didn't hear anything until you called for help, but *you* heard something. You heard the crack on Galen's head, even though you were a lot farther away."

"That's true," he said, and for the first time I heard hesitation in his voice. "But maybe Mia had her head in a closet or something."

"Then *who*?" I said, suddenly angry. "You were the one who said there wasn't anyone else harassing us, that the idea it was the Brummits was dumb, that it had to be one of us. So if it wasn't Galen and it wasn't Mia, who was it? And who killed Galen? Where did they go?"

"Maybe it was Galen all along," he said. "And then . . ."

"What?" I said, annoyed. "He fell and accidentally hit his head so hard you heard it, and then he died?" Even now, after everything that had happened, Liam was still trying to find a way to blame Galen.

"Okay, okay, it's stupid," Liam said. "So what's your explanation?"

I didn't say anything, I just glared at him. I'd already *told* him my explanation.

"It's not Mia," Liam said. "She's my best friend."

"Maybe he did attack her, like we were worried about," I said, "and she fought back."

"And she didn't say anything to us?"

"Maybe she's scared the police will blame her for what happened. Or maybe it was the two of them together, playing pranks, but something went wrong and Galen was going to tell us the truth, and Mia lost her temper."

"That doesn't sound like the Mia I know at all," Liam said.

The Mia he knew didn't keep secrets and tell lies? She wasn't a loose cannon? Did he and I know the same Mia?

"Think back," I said. "Where was Mia exactly when you found Galen's body?"

"In the cabin. Just like she said."

"How long before she appeared?"

"As soon as I shouted."

"Did she have anything in her hand?"

"Rob—"

"Liam, just think, okay? Anything you remember."

He mulled it over, but then shook his head. "She wasn't carrying anything. You would've seen it too. You showed up right after she did. And doesn't that prove she didn't do it? She didn't have anything to do it *with*."

"So maybe she attacked him, but then went back inside the cabin to hide the weapon. Or threw it in the woods."

"That doesn't make any sense at all," he said. "She didn't know we were following them. She thought you and I were still back here. At that point, she didn't have any reason to hide the weapon. The only thing that fits is exactly what she told us."

I stared at him, thinking. All this crazy speculation, trying to get everything right in my mind, had given me a headache. But Liam was definitely making sense again. It didn't make me angry this time. Mia not being the killer, that was a *good* thing. I'd jumped to another conclusion.

"So what then?" I said. There was no point to this whole conversation unless we figured out what to do next.

"You should change your clothes. You're all muddy. And you smell like piss."

I sighed and crossed to my bag, near the base of the ladder to the sleeping loft. I kicked off my shoes and changed my shirt.

Something nagged at me.

I turned and looked over at Mia's jacket, the one she'd taken off after poking the fire. She'd laid it over the back of the chair.

I glanced over at the door to the bedroom, where Mia had gone to be with Galen's body. It was still closed, with Mia inside.

I stepped toward the jacket. I was already fifty percent sure of what I'd find there.

"What are you doing?" Liam said.

"Nothing," I said as I reached for a pocket. "Just a hunch."

Almost as soon as I touched the jacket, I felt the weight of something in that pocket, something heavy.

I reached in and pulled out a handgun, big and heavy.

I turned it around in my hand, holding it by the muzzle, showing it to Liam. The butt of the handle was circular, about the size of a quarter.

Exactly the size of the wound on the back of Galen's head.

"What are you doing?" came a voice from the bedroom door.

Of course it was Mia, and of course she'd seen me finding the gun. Liam looked back and forth between us.

"You have a gun," I said. It was black, sleek, and sort of blocky, with a grip on the handle that was made out of some kind of rubber padding. I assumed the gun had some kind of safety, but even so I kept my finger as far from the trigger as possible. I didn't want to accidently set it off.

"Sure," she said as if it was incredibly obvious. "That's why we went over to the Brummits' cabin, remember?"

"Why didn't you say anything?"

"What do you mean?" She stepped away from the bedroom, leaving the door open behind her.

"You found a gun," I said. "You don't think that was kind of important information?"

"Well, it's not like I had anything else on my mind—like, oh, the fact that I'd just found my boyfriend dead."

I blushed. So much for my playing Sherlock Holmes.

"There was a rifle," she said, "but it was locked up in a case. I found the pistol in the nightstand."

"Is it loaded?" Liam asked.

"It is now," Mia said. She pulled something from her back pocket and tossed it onto the kitchen table with the other equipment—it landed with a bright rattle, almost like a jingle bell. A Ziploc plastic bag full of more ammo. "What?" she said, looking at Liam now.

He and I both had the same questions on our faces. Even with Galen dead, why didn't Mia tell us she'd found a gun? If she was armed, why had she acted all freaked out about someone being out there in the woods? If nothing else, why hadn't she put the gun on the kitchen table with the rest of our defenses? It almost seemed like she'd been hiding it. On the other hand, she really did have a lot on her mind. And if she was deliberately hiding it, wouldn't she have taken it into the bedroom with her?

But he didn't say any of this. Neither of us did.

Mia looked at me. "The real question," she said, "is what were you doing going through my jacket?"

I couldn't think of anything to say, any way to explain.

"It's just so strange," Liam said, "the way Galen died."

"So you think *I* did it?" The fuse to Mia's temper had instantly been lit.

"I don't know," Liam said. At first it surprised me that Liam didn't deny it, that he was being so open with her, but then it occurred to me that maybe honesty was the best policy. There had already been too much skulking around, too many secrets. Maybe it was time to get it all out into the open. No more lies.

Mia seemed to sense this too. Her short fuse quickly burned itself out. The explosion never came.

Liam explained how he and I thought that Galen had been the one pulling the pranks. As he talked, I glanced at the open door to the bedroom and thought about how Galen's dead body was still in there stretched out on the bed, growing colder by the minute.

Mia listened to Liam. She never once nodded, but she didn't get mad either.

"So?" Liam said once he was done. "What really happened over at that cabin?"

She hesitated. "Exactly what I told you," she said. "I didn't lie." Her body swayed slightly, like she was standing at the edge of a tall cliff. "Except for maybe one thing."

The floor creaked as Liam and I both shuffled our feet at the same time.

"Galen shoots up," she said. "He's been doing it as long as I've known him. I've told him I want him to stop, and I know he's going to, but he hasn't yet."

She was talking about him in the present tense, which was exactly what a person would do if they weren't that person's murderer. Then again, if a person was smart enough to pull off all the things that had happened, they were also probably smart enough to know that.

"Heroin?" Liam said.

"He called it antifreeze," Mia said. "But yeah."

"I didn't see any drugs," I said.

"Then you missed them," she said defiantly. "Or they're still in his pocket."

"So that's why he went outside while you were searching the cabin for the gun? To shoot up?"

"Probably. I don't like it when he does it around me, and he definitely didn't want you guys to see."

Galen being a heroin addict really did explain a lot of his behavior. His irritability in the afternoons at school, his breezy attitude the rest of the time, even his general bravado.

"Weren't you worried about someone hiding out in the woods?" I said.

"He didn't tell me he was doing it," Mia said. "He just left. I really didn't know he was gone."

"You think the drugs could've made Galen do all those things?" Liam asked. "The things that have been happening to us all weekend?" This hadn't occurred to me, but it made sense.

Mia shook her head. "No! I know you don't believe me, but he managed it. He never got out of control. Ever."

"He was out of control enough to leave the cabin alone in order to shoot up," I pointed out.

"It's not the same thing," Mia said. "Yeah, he had a problem with drugs, but he took it out on himself, not other people. He liked you guys. He never would've done these things." Mia looked at me. "You don't believe me that he used, do you? Needles don't leave tracks—that's a big misconception. Not unless you shoot up in the same place over and over. But if you look close, you can see the marks on his arms. He did it in his armpits a lot too." She nodded to the bedroom. "Go check. He kept his stash in a glasses case in the front of his coat."

I remembered the lump I'd felt in Galen's jacket, and the discoloration I'd seen under his arms when we'd gone skinny-dipping. And I remembered at the tattoo parlor, when those guys had chased us down that alley. That wasn't about Galen sleeping with that guy's girlfriend, it was about some drug deal gone bad.

Everything Mia said fit.

Even so, I said, "I don't know what to believe. I know someone's been jerking us around, and I know someone is now dead. Then you turn up with a weapon in your pocket that you didn't tell us about, after pretending we were still helpless victims. And when another part of your story doesn't make sense, you finally admit that your boyfriend is a drug addict."

I was sixty percent sure Mia was going to explode in anger, but once again she didn't. All she said was, "I didn't do it. And Galen didn't either."

"But you can't prove that," I said.

"I didn't know I had to."

"I'm looking for an explanation," Liam said. "That's all."

We all stood there, stock-still. Now the floor creaked under Mia's feet, but she didn't seem to have moved at all.

"I think we should leave," I said at last.

"Leave?" Mia said. "Leave where?"

I was confused. Hadn't Mia been the one who'd wanted to leave a few minutes before? I rubbed my face. My head was pounding, the headache worse than ever. I could feel both Mia and Liam staring at me.

"This cabin!" I said. "This whole place. We have a gun now.

We have protection." More specifically, *I* had the gun, and even if I had no idea how to use it, I wasn't giving it up.

"And go where?" she said.

"The highway," I said. "I don't know. Anywhere but here. There's something wrong with this place."

"But it's getting dark," Mia said, "and the sheriff will be here soon. I thought we were waiting for the sheriff."

"I don't care!" I said. "I just need to get out of here!"

I turned for the door, eager to throw it open.

"Wait," Mia said, stopping me. "I think I have one."

"One what?" Liam asked.

"An explanation. When we were in Marot, when we went in that sporting goods store, we lost track of Galen. I think maybe he did go outside. To make a score." As she talked, Mia crossed to the kitchen and poured herself a bowl of cereal with milk from the cooler.

"It was weird how fast he could always spot a dealer," Mia went on. "It's like they have some kind of secret code to iden-tify each other. Maybe it was those guys leaning against those cars. I mean, Marot is poor. It's desperate. It may not look like it, but it's exactly the kind of place where a lot of drug deals happen. But maybe it somehow went bad. Maybe Galen gave them some bills wrapped around some newsprint or something. Heroin is expensive, and Galen doesn't have a lot of money. Maybe the dealer was so angry that he and his friends followed us all the way up to this cabin. If they live around here, they'd probably know these woods better than anyone."

Liam and I listened. Another drug deal gone bad? It actually made sense. We knew from first-hand experience that Galen did things that really pissed dealers off.

But if drug dealers were the ones harassing us, if they were the ones who'd killed Galen, that meant they were still out there in the woods. Maybe they'd leave now that Galen was dead, but maybe they wouldn't. For all they knew, Galen was buying dope for the lot of us. And along with revenge, they probably also wanted their money.

"Then we're safer in here," I said. "Inside. We'd be crazy to try to walk for the road, especially in the dark." I was contradicting what I'd said before, but Mia's new theory changed everything.

"When did this stuff go stale?" Mia said, meaning the cereal. But she didn't stop eating it.

"We can seal the windows," Liam said. "Break off the doors to the kitchen cabinets and nail them over the windows." He nodded to the items on the kitchen table. "We have a hammer and nails. It might not keep them out if they really want to get inside, but it'll slow them down." He nodded at me, at the gun in my hand. "And now we have a gun."

I looked back at the front door. I knew I'd locked it, and it looked locked now, but I was tempted to check it to make sure. At least the dead bolt looked strong.

"We don't have to hold out forever," Mia said, gripping the bowl of cereal like it was a life preserver. "Just five or six hours."

Five or six hours? Suddenly that seemed like an eternity.

I put the gun on the table for the time being.

The first thing to do was seal the windows, like Liam had said. There were only three windows in all, two in the main room and one in the bedroom. The hardest part was getting the doors off the kitchen cabinets. We didn't have a screwdriver, so we had to tear them right off their hinges. The metal squealed like an animal dying. If there really was anyone outside watching us, they'd probably think we were in here torturing one another.

As we worked, my head throbbed. It wasn't just all the crazy thinking I'd been doing, it was everything: the tension of the situation, the squealing metal, and the sour smell of Galen's piss. Changing my shirt hadn't been enough. The stuff must have dried on my skin, and now that I was perspiring, it was stronger than ever. But I couldn't wash it off because there wasn't any running water in the cabin.

We sealed the windows in the front room first. The cabinet doors didn't cover the windows completely, but at least they'd stop anyone from trying to crawl inside. Then Liam and I headed into the bedroom while Mia stayed at the dinner table trying to figure out the mousetraps. If they worked okay, we could still set them around outside.

In the bedroom, I held the wood up to the window while Liam positioned the nail so he could start hammering.

Something clattered in the front room. Was it a mousetrap snapping, or something else?

Liam and I looked at each other.

"Mia?" I called.

Something scraped against the floor in the other room—a chair. Then it sounded like the chair fell over.

Mia gasped, almost like she was choking.

Liam and I ran to the doorway of the bedroom.

Mia had fallen to the floor by the dinner table. She was on her back, like a beetle that had been tipped over, her arms flailing, reaching for things she couldn't touch.

She was convulsing, literally foaming at the mouth.

It took a second for all this to make sense. Had she been shot? But the windows were mostly covered, and we hadn't heard any gunfire or breaking glass. Had someone come into the cabin and attacked her? My eyes found the dead bolt on the door, and it was still latched. Besides, except for Mia, the room was empty.

Liam and I ran to her side.

"Mia!" Liam said. "What's wrong?"

She tried to speak, or maybe to scream, but nothing came out of her mouth, just a white foam that bubbled up like a science experiment gone wrong. Unlike with Galen's dead body, this did look like it does in the movies. It was that weirdly perfect.

Did Mia have some disease I didn't know about, epilepsy or something? But Liam looked as surprised as me. So was she faking it?

She wasn't faking it. Her whole body began to twist. I'd never seen anyone move like that, flex and jerk into such weird positions, still on her back. Her eyes bulged, her face flushed impossibly red, and she gasped for air, desperate to breathe. She wasn't even trying to scream now.

Whatever this was, she was in terrible pain.

Liam and I tried everything to help her, to save her. We thought she might be choking on something, so we tried the Heimlich maneuver, but she pushed us away—or maybe it was her flailing. Then, thinking she was having some kind of seizure, we tried to hold her down, but she kept pulling away from us, thrashing about.

Finally, after what seemed like an hour but may have only been ten minutes, she whimpered. In a way, that was the most disturbing thing so far, because somehow I knew she knew it was all over.

She went rigid one final time, as stiff as a cupboard door, then fell completely slack. I won't say I could see the light leaving her eyes, because that also sounds too perfect, but that's almost the way it looked.

I checked for a pulse, and there wasn't one, like I knew there wouldn't be.

Mia was dead, and Liam and I were alone. But time did not stop now, or even slow. It just ticked on, second by second, propelling us both forward into whatever the hell was going to happen next.

For a long time, Liam and I stared down at Mia's lifeless body.

After Galen, I knew what a dead body looked like, how limp and lifeless it could be. That's what Mia looked like now. But she hadn't just fallen dead. Something had *happened* to her. Someone had *done* this. And whoever that someone was, they had to still be around.

But I had no idea what to do about any of this. It was like I was paralyzed.

Finally Liam said, "What the hell?"

That knocked me into motion. I stood up and walked to the door. Now I did check the lock, but everything was fine. The windows in the front room were still covered too.

So what had happened?

I looked down at Mia again, the pain and fear frozen on her face. But there were no answers there.

I noticed the spiderweb tattoo on her wrist, red and a little puffy, like it had become infected, or maybe it was only still healing. Not that it would ever heal now.

"Rob, what just happened?" Liam said louder. "How did she die?"

I looked around the room. Only now did I notice the box of rat poison on the table. I picked it up and read the back. The print was old and faded.

"Strychnine," Liam said. He stood behind me reading the ingredients on the box.

"What—?"

"It's a poison. A nasty one. I don't think it's used much anymore."

"But how—?" Even as I said this, I knew the answer: Mia's bowl of cereal. I turned to her dirty dish on the kitchen counter. Someone must have mixed the poison in with her cereal.

I looked inside the box of poison. There was still a little bit of rat poison left, dark and flaky, almost like wood shavings. I looked into the box of cornflakes, and even though I couldn't make out the rat poison, I knew there was some in there too. With everything mixed together, Mia wouldn't have seen it either. She'd said it had tasted stale.

I didn't say any of this to Liam. He already knew.

"Whoever killed Galen killed Mia too," I said. "They must have come into the cabin when we were over at the Brummits."

"Unless . . ." Liam said thoughtfully.

I looked at him.

"Galen," he said.

"What about him?"

"Maybe it was Galen who did this. Before he died. With everything going on, he had to know that Mia would have a bowl of cereal before too long. So he put the poison in her cereal."

"But then why did Mia kill him?"

"Because she found out what he'd been doing. That he was the one who'd been harassing us all along. They fought, and she killed him, and then she lied to us about the whole thing."

Somehow Liam had found a way to blame Galen after all.

But if he was right, it meant we were safe, that anyone who might harass or kill us was already dead. That all we had to do was wait a few more hours for the sheriff to arrive.

But what if he's not right? I thought. What if it was someone else who had done all these terrible things?

Liam and I kept staring at each other, not moving.

And then we did something I never in a million years thought I'd do in a situation like that.

We had sex.

First, Liam leaned over and kissed me.

I immediately kissed him back. I wasn't surprised by what he had done, not at all. It was like I'd been expecting it.

It was a passionate kiss, daring and desperate. As we kissed, our fingers fumbled with each other's buttons and zippers and elastic bands. Our hands roamed across each other's bare skin, over muscles, into crevices, stroking and squeezing, cupping and probing.

Clothes disappeared as if by magic. They were suddenly all around us on the floor.

Then we were naked together on that floor. Fields of skin

had appeared, hills and valleys to be explored with hands and tongues, even as we gasped and grunted and moaned. I followed trails of dark hair that led to forests of thatch. Things dripped, but not on me, not like in the rain forest. This time I tasted the moisture, Liam's sweat and more. I took it inside my mouth, savored its flavor, let it become part of me.

I honestly can't believe I'm telling you all this—I'm really embarrassed right now—but I think it's important for you to know, to understand exactly how I felt.

I was closer to dying than I'd ever been in my entire life, and I was closer to actual death than I'd ever been and probably ever will be until the day I die myself: there was a dead body in the bedroom and another one not five feet from us. The mud I'd tracked in from the rain forest surrounded us like Satanic symbols painted on the floor.

But I'd never felt more alive. Galen's and Mia's bodies were dead and limp and sagging, but not Liam and me. Our bodies were firm and taut and throbbing. Everything that could be hard was hard, everything soft was tender and vulnerable. All the blood that flowed was warm and alive.

It was the hottest sex I've ever had in my life—hotter than my first time with Liam, hotter than that night up in the loft. It'll probably be the hottest sex I ever *will* have, but it wasn't necessarily because of anything we did.

It was why we were doing it, what it meant.

Mia and Galen were dead, but Liam and I weren't. And through this complicated ritual called sex, this magic spell that we somehow instinctively knew the motions to, we could ward off death, keep it at bay, no matter how close by it might be. And the louder we grunted, the harder and deeper we thrust against each other, into each other, the farther we pushed the darkness away.

At least until we were done. We went on like that for at least half an hour, but eventually our bodies exploded in release. Our heartbeats slowed, and our bodies relaxed. We were still alive, the blood was still flowing, but everything was back like it was before.

When it came to death, all bets were off again.

I looked over at Liam, spent and naked on the floor. No words were needed to say what I was feeling, how satisfied I was, how close I felt to him. We'd been so in sync before, often knowing what the other was thinking, but it hadn't been like this. It had never occurred to me that human beings could even *be* this close. All that talk people do about sex and love, about people becoming one? Until now, I'd always thought it was just so many words, some kind of stupid metaphor. But it didn't feel like a metaphor now. The sex had made us one, and even though the sex was over, it was like we were still one person, sharing all the very same thoughts and fears, with no distance or barriers between us. And I knew it was the danger we were in, all the things that had happened, that had made us this way. Did that make the whole experience worthwhile?

Not unless we survived, it didn't.

From my spot on the floor, I could see up under the dinner table. There were spiderwebs there too, lots of them, thick and silvery. There were more webs under the chairs. I thought we'd gotten them all on Friday night, but we hadn't, not even close.

Liam sat upright. "We should go."

I sat upright too. "You want to leave the cabin?"

He nodded. "We're not safe here. We never were. Even if Galen did poison the cereal for Mia, who's to say that's the only trap he left? Maybe there's a bomb in the fireplace. Maybe he cut some beam and the whole roof's about to collapse."

"But—" I began.

"—we don't know the roads?" he finished. "We can take our chances. Besides, we know the direction of the main highway. We can cut through the forest if we have to. It can't be more than ten miles."

"But what if—?"

"—there really is someone out there waiting for us? Well, if we stay here, they know exactly where we are. And besides—"

"—we still have the gun."

I met him smile for smile.

Like I said, Liam and I were one.

The tin cans with the nails inside rattled quietly when we opened the door.

Night had fallen, and the moon, if there was one, was still hidden behind soggy clouds. But we didn't dare dig for the flashlights in our backpacks for fear that we'd be obvious in the dark. We started for the road.

Hidden pots jangled and clattered in the ferns all around us. We'd forgotten about the fishing line that Mia had strung around the yard—Galen's alarm system—and now we were hopelessly entangled in it. Mia had been right when she'd said it would be invisible in the dark. Now we'd called more attention to ourselves than if we'd just turned on our flashlights.

Once free from the fishing line, we started up the dirt road. The mud wasn't as bad as earlier in the day, but we still needed to walk on the rocky bulge in the middle of the road, and that meant going single file. I went first, and Liam followed, walking in my footsteps. I had the gun, and it felt unnaturally heavy in my hand, like it was made of lead or gold.

At least the rain was holding off.

We walked for a long time without either of us saying anything. The only sound was the crunch of rocks under our feet, and the dripping of water in the trees all around us. I was so sick of the rain forest and the Chinese water torture of its endless drip, drip, drip. I kept imagining I could feel someone watching me, their eyes trained on my every move. But no one could've been watching me all that time. It was impossible. To do it, they'd have to be able to fly, or somehow move silently through the trees.

Before long, the rain forest came to an end. The meandering desolation of the clear-cut stretched out in front of us. Once again, the mud was worse here with no trees to block the rain.

I stopped, scanning the flattened landscape. Before, I'd felt comforted by the clear-cut, by the fact that there was no place for anyone to hide. But it was dark now, the perfect camouflage. Maybe our stalkers had night-vision gunsights—I'd seen some of those in the sporting goods store. And whether it was the Brummits or drug dealers, they probably had guns too.

"It's going to be okay," Liam said softly.

I nodded in the darkness. I wanted to believe him, but I was less than twenty percent sure he was right.

I didn't smell Galen's piss anymore. Now it was Liam I smelled on my skin, the lingering musk of the sex we'd shared. That made me feel a little better.

I started forward again, gravel crunching. My palm sweated against the grip of the gun in my hand.

Halfway across the clear-cut, Liam asked me, "When was the last time you thought you might die?"

I knew what he was thinking by asking me this. He had all the same scary thoughts I did about what might happen to us. And if we had them, why not say them out loud? It was like how doctors in the Middle Ages used to drill holes in the heads of those they thought were possessed by demons: better to let the demons out into the open air than have them knocking around inside our skulls.

"I had a sore throat last year," I said. "It was really, really bad. It hurt so bad just to swallow that I couldn't eat, I couldn't even drink. I kept getting sicker and sicker until I could hardly breathe. I had to go to the emergency room. The doctor told me that I was dehydrated and put me on an IV drip. Then he told me that if I hadn't come to the emergency room when I did, if I'd waited even a few more hours, my throat probably would've closed completely, and I would've suffocated."

Liam nodded in the dark. I felt kind of stupid that, until now, the closest I'd come to dying was a really bad sore throat.

"What about you?" I asked.

"I was on a plane once when it lost power," he said. "For a while, we were in free fall. Everyone, all the passengers, thought we were going to die."

"Really? That must've been terrifying."

"It was. But it wasn't like this. Like now."

"How was it different?"

"Because we were powerless. There was nothing any of us could do to stop it."

I smiled. "And that's different from now, how exactly?"

"The difference," he said, "is that we're the ones in control now. And if we run into the person who did all this to us, we're going to make him pay."

His voice was so strong and confident, even next to the vast emptiness of the clear-cut. It actually gave me chills.

I've been saying all along—I'd *thought* all along—that Liam and I were so much alike, so much in a sync. But that wasn't entirely true. Maybe Galen had been an alpha, determined to be in charge, but in his fussy, nervous way, Liam was an alpha too. He was much less obvious about it than Galen, but when it came to the big things, he knew exactly what to do, and he usually got his way. Why hadn't I seen it before? He had this quiet certainty that was almost breathtaking. Maybe that's why he'd butted heads with Galen in the first place—because they were two alphas. But there was no conflict with me, because I had no problem letting him be more dominant. In fact, I liked it, especially right then. It was comforting, sexy even, knowing he was there with me, that he knew what to do, that he seemed so unstoppable. But it didn't mean we weren't still connected in a very real way, that we weren't two halves of some kind of a single whole. Don't they say that with twins there is always one dominant one?

I'd told him before that I could see what he saw in Mia, but now I saw what Mia saw in him, why she'd ended up being best friends with him. He was like Galen, and she was attracted to that. Meanwhile, I was like Mia, less dominant, at least underneath where it mattered. That was probably why it had taken Mia and me so long to warm up to each other. Aren't we usually drawn to our opposites? Don't we sometimes clash the most with those who are most like us?

It all made perfect sense.

I kept walking forward. Up ahead, the clear-cut came to an end. We were approaching the rain forest again, that towering black wall. It looked even darker in the night.

But Liam had given me my focus back, made me clear-headed again. Knowing that he was behind me, that he had my back, I followed the road into the forest.

The branches of the trees interweaved over our heads. It really was like a cave.

It was almost too dark to see, but I still didn't dare turn on the flashlight, at least not yet, so close to the opening behind us. Of course water dribbled down from above. I could still smell Liam on my skin, and right then it felt like no matter how much water dribbled down from the moss and trees above, it could never wash that wonderful scent off me.

Two sets of feet crunched on the gravel in the rise in the middle of the road.

But then there was only one set of feet.

"Liam?" I said, turning behind me.

He wasn't there.

"Liam?" I said again, too confused to be scared. Had he gone off to pee? Why hadn't he said anything?

Now I *was* scared. The fear filled me in a flash, like compressed air into a life raft. I could barely breathe or even move.

I remembered the gun in my hand. I forced it upright, pointing it around me, even as I somehow fumbled in my backpack for the flashlight.

"Liam, this isn't funny!"

I finally found my light. I turned it on, slicing the misty forest with its beam. But I didn't see Liam anywhere.

He'd been right behind me on the road, so I took a couple of steps back, searching the undergrowth with my light.

Liam was splayed out, back against the ferns, lifeless.

Someone had cut his throat.

There was blood everywhere, all over the front of his shirt and jacket. But it all started at his throat. He'd been garroted. The slash was deep and terrible.

"Liam!" I ducked down to his side. He was propped upright, held in place by the vegetation. But it didn't look anything like he was sitting normally because his head was lolling backward into the ferns. That's what made the cut on his throat so obvious.

I put my fingers up to the wound on his neck, trying to staunch the flow of blood, but there was too much of it. It was everywhere, warm and sticky. It was all over his body, and now all over me. The smell was stronger than it had been with Galen, probably because there was more of it. It was this metallic, meaty tang that hung in the air, lingering in my sinuses.

His body was still warm, but it wouldn't be for long. I'd seen death twice before, and now I knew how it worked.

Even so, this wasn't like Mia and Galen's dying. Those were both terrible tragedies, but I'd barely known the two of them. This was Liam, my boyfriend. Seconds before, I'd been thinking of him as part of me.

I'd also been thinking of him as unstoppable, but I couldn't have been more wrong.

I was still afraid—terrified. But it was different now. Nothing made any sense. Without Liam, I felt lost.

Who had done it? I jerked around, twitchy, like a fish fearful of the eagle that might be circling overhead, out of sight. Was the killer out in the forest, watching me even now? At first I assumed he had to be. But then I wondered if maybe we'd walked into some kind of trap—a taut wire stung between the trees, like the fishing lines Mia had stretched out across the yard. I looked around, pointed the flashlight everywhere, but I didn't see anything. If it really was a trap, why hadn't it affected me? Was it some kind of sharp pendulum that had swung in from the trees?

The better question was what did I do now?

I lifted the gun again even as I swept the flashlight around in a circle. Droplets of water slithered through the beam like bacteria in a microscope. I heard irregular taps all around me as the water hit the undergrowth.

I didn't *know* Liam had been killed by a trap, so I called out. "Who are you? Show yourself!"

No one stepped forward or said anything from the trees, just like I knew they wouldn't.

I couldn't stay where I was. I was a total sitting duck.

But what about Liam? I couldn't leave him here in the woods.

I shone my light down at him again. He stared up at the trees with marble eyes. Blood dripped from his neck down to the ground. It was barely falling two feet, but I swear I could hear it as it hit the moss. Blood was thicker than water.

With Galen, I'd carried him back to the cabin on my shoulders. But how could I do that with Liam? I still had miles and miles to go before I even reached the highway, and I now knew for a fact someone was stalking me.

I'm not proud of what I did next. Liam was my boyfriend,

and I loved him. And after everything that had happened to us this weekend, I really had felt like we were more connected than ever.

But now he was dead. That half of me, maybe even the dominant half, was gone.

So I panicked. With no one to tell me what to do, no quiet confidence guiding me calmly through the rain forest, I did the only thing I could think of.

I ran.

At first I continued down the logging road, fumbling in the darkness, sliding in the mud. But then I remembered how Liam had been killed. What if it *had* been some kind of trap that had been set for us? Did that mean there might be more traps ahead?

I turned and broke into the rain forest, in what I thought was the direction of the highway. Yes, maybe this was exactly what the killer expected me to do—maybe there was a trap waiting for me in here somewhere too—but I was tired of trying to understand someone I couldn't see, someone I'd never even met.

I ran through the forest. The ground was irregular, sloping downward, and the undergrowth was thick. I tripped on logs and vines, but the devil's walkingstick was the worst. I ran into branches and stalks, their spiky thorns tearing at my clothes and skin. After one really nasty patch, I even stopped and considered going back to Liam's body. If they'd killed him, they might as well get me too. But the cold, clear water that dripped down from above almost felt good now, soothing the hot scratches on my skin. Maybe it did finally feel like a baptism. In the end, I worked my way through the thorns and kept running.

I burst out of the forest into a clear-cut. Even now, I was surprised and disoriented by the disappearance of the trees. The smell of mud was back, but this clear-cut was so fresh that I could also smell the sap seeping from the tree stumps like blood. With all the stumps in front of me, the ground was even more irregular than before. If I kept running, I was certain to trip and fall.

A single tree stood in the field in front of me, about thirty feet away.

Or *was* it a tree? The moon was still behind the clouds, and a mist hung in the air, obscuring everything. It was about the width of a tree, and it stood upright. But it had no branches, and the whole thing was oddly shaped and only about seven feet tall. It was too tall to be a stump, but not tall enough to be a full tree. Why would the loggers leave half a tree?

Unless it wasn't a tree.

Maybe it's a man, I thought.

If it was a man, he was very tall, seven feet at least. He'd also have to be holding his arms against his body. But maybe the silhouette was rounded on top because that was his head.

If it was a man, he was staring in my direction. If it was a man, it was as if he'd been standing there waiting for me.

I wished I had my flashlight, but I'd dropped that and my backpack back on the road. I knew there was at least one other person in this woods other than me, and I also knew I didn't want to run into him.

"Is there someone there?" I said. I expected my voice to echo in the open field, but it didn't.

The tree didn't move.

"I mean it!" I said. "Answer me!"

It didn't answer.

The highway was on the other side of this tree, still miles and miles away. I could try to walk around it, to the right or back toward the road, but what was the point? If that really was a person standing in the middle of the field, he already knew I was there.

I started forward, weaving between stumps. The smell of sap was overwhelming. Somehow I could sense its stickiness, like the whole clear-cut was trying to stop me, trap me like an insect in flypaper. Or maybe it was the sticky blood on my arms and hands.

When I was twenty or so feet away, the tree moved.

It *was* a man. He stepped down off something, a stump probably, which had made him look a lot taller than he was.

He wasn't any taller than me. I could see the body more clearly now, how perfect his posture was. But in the darkness, I still couldn't see his face. Or maybe it was a she, not a he—I couldn't see clearly enough to make that out either. I'd only assumed it was a guy because they looked so tall.

The person walked toward me. Mud squished underfoot. My fear was back, stronger than ever, filling me, paralyzing me again.

"Stop!" I said. "Don't come any closer!"

The figure didn't stop. It kept walking right toward me, until he was finally close enough for me to make out his face.

"Hello, Rob," he said quietly.

It was Liam.

"Liam?" I said. "What are you *doing* here?" Closer now, I could see that he was still drenched with blood. The gash on his neck was deep and sickening.

"What does it look like I'm doing?" he said.

"But . . . you were dead. I saw your body. I felt your blood!"

He reached up and peeled the cut right off his neck. He held it up like a discarded snakeskin. How was that possible?

"I thought that was a nice touch," he said matter-of-factly. "And the warm blood? Know how I did that? A pouch strapped to my body. It's real blood, by the way. Mine. I thought I might need it, so I brought the equipment and drew it this morning. When I strapped it on right before we left the cabin, my body heated it to exactly the right temperature. Wasn't that clever?"

"Why would you fake your own death?" Was this some

way he'd thought of to outwit whoever was harassing us? No. Even as I was speaking, the pieces of the puzzle were falling into place in my mind.

It had been Liam all along. He'd killed Galen. He could've slipped the hammer from the kitchen table into his jacket right before we followed Galen and Mia to the Brummits'. Then when I got stuck in that patch of devil's walkingstick, he'd hurried on ahead to the Brummits' cabin. Mia had been inside, but Galen had gone outside to shoot up. Liam had snuck up on him from behind.

And he'd put the rat poison in the cereal too, knowing that Mia would pour herself a bowl eventually.

But none of this made any sense! Liam was the one who had suggested that the harasser was one of us in the first place. More than that, I loved him. And he loved me. We were one.

Weren't we?

"It was you," I said. "All along."

"Of course it was me," he said. "Who else could it have been? Mia and Galen are both dead. The Brummits? That was always such a stupid theory. A drug deal gone bad? Better, but what kind of small town drug dealer do you think is smart enough to pull all this off?"

"But . . . why?"

"Why do you think? You already know the answer. You learned it this weekend. It surprised me that it even came up."

I thought back. What had I learned this weekend that would possibly explain why Liam would kill his best friend and her boyfriend?

"Come on," he said. "Think it through."

"I *am* thinking it through!" I said. "I don't know what you're talking about!"

"Here's a clue. Think about Mia's lie."

"Her what?"

"During the game. Three Truths and a Lie? She said it was a lie, but you and I both knew it was the truth."

"The man she hit on the bike?"

Liam smiled. And then I knew he'd been awake in the loft, pretending to snore while Mia and I had talked. He'd heard everything we said.

"But what does . . ." I took another look at Liam. It was no man Mia had hit, and he hadn't died in the hit-and-run, like she'd thought. "That was you?" In the dark, Mia had mistaken a boy for a man.

He didn't need to nod. I already knew I was right. It seemed I'd mistaken a man for a boy. An angry, psychotic boy.

"But she was your friend," I said. "Why didn't you say anything? How did she not know?"

He looked off into the night. "When it happened, she wasn't my friend yet. I did tutor her, like I told you. But I'd made a point to be her tutor. Like I made a point to become her friend. Her *best* friend. That night she hit me with her car, she could've killed me. She sent me to the hospital, to six months of physical therapy. I told my parents I lost control of my bike. I never told anyone what really happened, or that when Mia stopped, I saw her face."

I tried to make sense of what he was saying. "She almost killed you, left you to die, and then you deliberately went on to become friends with her?"

He looked back at me and smiled again. His teeth glowed white in the dark.

"And you never told her?" I said.

"Why would I tell her? The whole point was to wait."

"For what?"

"For the perfect moment."

I couldn't believe what I was hearing.

"You mean you pretended to be her friend all these years, just so you'd have a chance for a weekend like this? For a chance to make her pay?"

"You said it yourself," he said. "What do we really have in common? You never liked Mia. Truth is, I never liked her either. You know what really got me? That she was alone that night. It might've been different if she'd been out driving with friends—if they'd scared or shamed her into leaving the scene. I can almost understand that. But she was alone. Her decision to leave me was entirely her own. What kind of person does that?"

His words dripped down over me, covering me, sliding down my face, into the neck of my shirt, down my back, all the way down to my underwear. But they weren't like water, or even piss. They were like sap, viscous and sticky, coating me, hardening into amber. How could I have been with someone for three months and not have seen this? What kind of split personality did he have? Did he ever care about me at all?

"You'll never get away with this," I said, realizing what a cliché it was even as I said it. "Two people are dead. You don't think the police will come out here and look for evidence?"

"There's no evidence that will tie anything to me. There *is* evidence that will tie it to a mysterious someone else. I planted it. I'll have to injure myself before the police come. I'll need a real reason for all this blood."

Was he telling the truth? It was obvious that he'd been several steps ahead of me the whole time. Liam was more dominant, more certain of himself, than even I knew. He truly was unstoppable.

"But . . . ," I said. "How could you even know we'd come out here? It was Galen's idea to come to this cabin. And it was my idea to go away in the first place!"

"People are easier to manipulate than you think," Liam said. "But mostly it was just a question of being adaptable. Of changing to fit the circumstances."

I tried to think, but the sap was seeping into my brain now. Even my thoughts were sticky.

"Okay," I said, forcing words out. "I understand why you killed Mia. But why Galen? He never did anything to you." *And why me?*

He shrugged. "To make her pay. She really loved him, you know. But also because he was a real prick." So that part of it wasn't a lie—the part about Galen teasing Liam, and Liam hating him in return. Liam said, "And you're also thinking, 'What about me?'"

Even now, we were thinking the same thoughts.

"You know," he said, "I was going to let you live."

Was? I thought.

"You seemed so genuinely upset by Mia's story. By what she had done."

"I was," I said. "I am! It's horrible what she did to you!" At this point, I was going to tell Liam whatever he wanted to hear. But how much had he heard the night before? Had he understood how much I'd started to see things from Mia's point of view?

"But."

"What?" I said. I heard the panic in my voice, even only speaking that single word.

"Don't you see? I gave you a chance to see if you were any different. And it turns out you weren't."

"A chance? What are you talking about?"

"Ten minutes ago. Back on the trail. If you'd tried to save me, I was going to let you live. If you'd started to carry me to the highway, I was going to come to and we would've continued on, and you never would've known the truth."

"I thought you were dead. You *looked* dead!"

"Did you check my pulse? Even I can't stop my own heart. But you didn't even check. You assumed I was dead and ran like the coward you are. Which proved to me that you're no different than Mia. That you're just as weak. You were alone too, so it was a test of the real you. But you failed. When things get tough, when push comes to shove, you only think of yourself."

"Liam, I love you, and I thought you loved me. That wasn't all a lie. I know it wasn't."

"No," he said. "It wasn't all a lie."

"Then let's work this out. No one knows what happened

up here except you and me. You say there's no evidence that you did this? You think I'm going to tell on you? I won't!"

He stared at me, thinking. "You'd do that for me?"

"Yes!" I said. "I would! I *will*!"

"But Rob, I don't believe you. Unfortunately, you're not a very good liar. Remember the game?"

"I'll do better! You can teach me how to lie better!"

"But how do I know you'd keep your word? How do I know you wouldn't tell the police everything?"

"I wouldn't! I promise!"

"Except I already know you're lying. That's how bad a liar you are. Besides, I already gave you a chance to do something for me, back there on the trail, and you blew it."

"I didn't know!" I said. "I'm sorry. Give me another chance."

"That's the thing about character tests, Rob. They only work when you don't know you're being tested. Otherwise they're meaningless. They can be faked. You can lie your way through."

So that was it? Liam had already made up his mind? He was going to kill me anyway?

"You're forgetting something," I said.

"What's that?" he said.

"I'm still the one with the gun." Unlike the flashlight, I'd kept a tight grip on the weapon as I ran through the woods. I was still holding it in my hand, thick and heavy.

I pointed it at Liam and flicked the switch to unhook the safety. I'd never held a gun before, but it was obvious how to unlock it, so intuitive.

Liam's eyes widened in the dark. They were even whiter than his teeth.

"If you really think you can shoot me in cold blood, then do it," he said. "But you forget I've spent the last three months with you. I know you, Rob. How you think. I know you can't do it."

Liam thought he was so good at reading my mind? He wasn't, not at all.

I pulled the trigger.

The gun clicked. It didn't shoot.

I fired again. Empty.

Liam laughed. "Did you really think I wouldn't take the

bullets out of the magazine? It was easy enough back in the cabin when you were getting dressed. And now I've given you another test, just like you asked, and you failed it. You proved once again how much like Mia you are. And you also proved that everything you said to me now was a lie."

What could I say? Liam was absolutely right.

He was still laughing. He sounded different now, like a completely different person, like someone I'd never even met. He'd said our relationship hadn't been a complete lie, but it had. Nothing but an endless stream of lies and only one single truth, right now at the very end.

Liam lifted a stick or a baton. He'd had it at his side, in his left hand. Liam was left-handed. I'd known that, of course: he and Mia were *both* left-handed, but it had never occurred to me to suspect Liam.

It was a Taser wand. I could see the two small electrodes at the very end. He must have snuck it in with him this weekend.

He took a step forward. "I'm not sure what to do with your body," he said. "How to explain what happened here in the woods. But I'll think of something."

"You're really going to kill me?" Even after everything, I couldn't quite believe it.

"Yes," he said, and it didn't take any skill at all to know he was finally telling me the whole, complete truth.

21

I turned and ran. The mud squished under my feet. For Liam to get me, he first needed to touch me with that Taser. So I knew he'd follow.

And he did. Mud sloshed behind me.

But I wasn't planning on running from him. The second he started after me, I stopped and turned on him. Brilliant mastermind or not, he hadn't been expecting that.

I came at him on his right side, the one where he wasn't holding the Taser. He wasn't expecting that either.

He gasped in surprise as I grabbed him and threw him to the ground. His head just missed one of the freshly cut stumps. This close to the ground, the smell of pine and sap was overwhelming.

"Stop!" he said. "No!"

He squirmed, but I held on, pinning him down. We were both slick with blood, and as we wrestled, it mixed together, like blood brothers. Except it wasn't really like that, since it was all the same blood, his blood. The Taser wand was attached to his wrist with a cord, but I held his hand down, my knee pressed right into his little spiderweb tattoo.

Still he fought back. Liam and I were the same size, but he was stronger, more sure of himself, the dominant one. I was determined to overpower him, but I wasn't even fifty percent sure I could.

We fought. He yanked his hand out from under my knee, and I felt us roll, then he was on top of me. We kept fighting, and it reminded me of the sex we'd had earlier in the cabin. Like then, we flexed and grunted and twisted. Sweat dripped off both of us, and I could smell his musk, heady and intoxicating.

But this wasn't sex. It was the opposite of sex. Sex was about life. This was about death.

We kept wrestling, both of us groaning, and suddenly I found myself sitting on his chest again. He may have been the dominant one, but I was winning this fight. I was stronger, at least at that moment. I guess I wanted it more.

Liam squirmed underneath me again, writhing and gasping. But somehow I pinned both his hands with my knees.

My hands encircled his neck and I began to squeeze.

I said before I'm not proud of what I did on the road, leaving Liam behind like that. I'm not proud of what I did here either. Could I have grabbed the Taser and subdued him? Given him a chance to surrender? Maybe I could have. But the truth is I didn't even try. So maybe Liam was right about me. Maybe I did think of myself first.

With my hands around his neck, I squeezed the life right out of him. It wasn't like with Mia where I could actually see the light disappear from her eyes. It was too dark for that. But I could *feel* Liam dying, like his soul was struggling along with his body, desperate to stay inside, but it was slowly being pulled out, like a snail out of its shell.

At the start of this story, I decided to tell you the whole truth about what happened that weekend, no matter how shocking or embarrassing.

So I guess I have to tell you that at the exact moment when Liam died, when he fell limp for good, when whatever soul he had finally left his body . . .

I liked it.

The truth is I'd never felt so powerful in my whole entire life. Liam was stoppable after all, and I'd been the one to do it.

But it was still self-defense. If anyone had ever deserved to die more than Liam, I'm not sure who.

I felt him below me, lifeless. Once before, he'd fooled me with limp muscles and a glassy-eyed look. I thought I'd known what death looked like, but I hadn't. But this time it was no act. I felt for his pulse. He really was dead.

I stood up, dizzy. My headache was back, even worse than before, but I ignored it. At first I looked away from him, from his body. But I didn't leave. I had to see him one last time, the person I'd been so sure was the other half of me.

I stared at him for so long I lost track of time. At some point, the moon finally broke through the clouds. Liam looked so familiar and yet so alien, and it had nothing to do with the fact that he was dead. He and I weren't the same. We never had been.

We couldn't have been more different.

Eventually I turned away. But I could still smell his musk on me, stronger than ever. I knew I'd be smelling it for a long time to come.

I staggered through that clear-cut, toward the highway, past stumps bleeding sap and through pools and streams of clouded water. There must have been mud in my shoes rubbing against my skin, and I'm sure the water was cold, but I have no memory of any of that.

Before long, the clear-cut ended, and I came to another patch of forest. I slogged on through that too, over soggy ferns and angry thorns, all of which I ignored. And then there was another clear-cut, and another patch of rain forest, and on and on, back and forth, all through the night.

Eventually I came to the highway, and I flagged a passing car. The driver called the police on his cell phone.

It wasn't for at least another hour after that, until I was finally in the hospital in Marot, that I relaxed, even a little. But Liam was dead, and I was safe.

It was all finally over, and I alone had survived.

I'd finished my story.

The doctor stared at me, but I honestly couldn't tell what he was thinking. I was in a single bed, and he was sitting in a chair facing me. The air smelled like disinfectant from the floors and bleach from the sheets. I wasn't wearing a hospital gown. It was more like a pair of pajamas.

"That's quite a story," he said.

"You're telling me," I said. "If it hadn't happened to me, I'm not sure I'd believe it."

"Really?"

"Would you? If it happened to you, I mean?" I scratched my nose.

"Tell me something," the doctor said softly.

"What's that?"

"You're left-handed too, aren't you?"

I had to think about that for a second, but then I realized that yes, I was left-handed.

"So?" I said.

"That's quite a coincidence, don't you think? Everyone except for Galen being left-handed?"

"I guess so. But what difference does that make?" I looked around the room. It didn't look like an ordinary hospital. It was more like a dormitory, except the door had a small window. "Where am I anyway? I don't remember this place."

"It's a place for you to get better," he said. "Liam."

"What?" I said, confused. "My name's not Liam. It's Rob." I laughed. "Haven't you been listening to anything I've said?"

"Yes, I've been listening. I've been listening very closely. You've told me the same story for eight days in a row. I've heard it all again and again."

"No, you haven't!" I said. I felt groggy. Had I been drugged? Even if I hadn't, I'd gone through an incredibly traumatic experience. Anyone would be confused after something like that. Still, what he said about my having told the story before did have the ring of truth. "Have you?" I asked.

The doctor nodded. "I have, Liam."

"Why do you keep calling me that?" I said, irritated. "That's not my name."

"But it is."

"No, I'm *Rob*. Rob Gear."

"Like that brand of camouflage gear in the sporting goods store?"

"What? No. That was just a coincidence."

"Rob Gear isn't your name. Your name is Liam Linard."

I laughed again, even if it didn't seem quite so funny this time. Plus, the laughter sounded familiar somehow. Where had I heard it before?

"Then who is Rob Gear?" I said.

"Rob Gear doesn't exist. He never did. You made him up."

"Of course Rob exists! He's me. Are you saying I don't exist?"

"I'm saying you're not Rob. There is no Rob. You're Liam Linard, and you spent the weekend two weeks ago at a cabin in the rain forest with your best friend, Mia, and her boyfriend, Galen. And you killed them both. But after you'd done it, while you were still out in those woods, you created some kind of alter ego. I don't know when exactly—maybe it was right after you killed Mia or maybe it was a little later—but you told the police and everyone at the hospital that your name was Rob Gear, that you'd been a victim of Liam's, along with the others. You were quite convincing. It took a long time, and a lot of people, to piece it all together."

I leaned back, and the bed squeaked. "That doesn't make sense. Why would I lie? Think it through."

"Tell me this then," the doctor said. "If everything happened the way you said it did . . ."

If? I honestly didn't understand why the doctor didn't believe me.

"Why do you have that tattoo?" the doctor finished.

"What?" I said.

"On your wrist."

I was curious, but both my hands were in my lap now, facing down. I didn't move them. But I felt a tingle, a little itch, right where Liam, Mia, and Galen had all gotten their tattoos.

"Go on," the doctor said. "Take a look."

I turned my wrist over. Sure enough, I had a tattoo now. It was a little spiderweb, exactly like the ones the others had gotten. What in the world? How had that gotten there?

"I thought you said you didn't get a tattoo," the doctor said. "So how did that get there?"

I had to think. How *had* it gotten there? We definitely left the tattoo parlor before I had a chance to get one.

"Liam!" I said at last. "He must've done it to me at some point during the night."

"And you didn't wake up?" the doctor said. "And you never noticed it until right now?"

The tattoo itched more intensely now. It almost burned, but I didn't dare scratch it. I turned my hand over again and buried it in the sheets.

"Did Liam put you up to this?" I said at last. "Is he behind all this?" I squirmed again, but this time the bed didn't squeak. It didn't even move. I must have jogged it up against the wall.

"That's a pretty elaborate prank," the doctor said. "Besides, I thought Liam was dead. You said you were sure."

I froze. How could I have forgotten that? "That's right. Still. I told you all the things he did. He anticipates—*anticipated*—everything."

"You did anticipate everything," the doctor said. "Mia and Galen's every move. But you didn't anticipate how you yourself would react. That by the time the police arrived, you'd have invented this person called Rob to deal with the guilt of killing your best friend and her boyfriend. And now you keep telling me the same elaborate story over and over again, in an effort to convince yourself it really happened the way you said it did. It's like what you said Mia told you: it's a psychological game you're playing to convince yourself a lie is the truth."

"But I *didn't* kill Mia and Galen," I said. "*Liam* did."

"And you killed Liam?"

"*Yes!* In self-defense, but yes. In the woods."

"There were two bodies at the cabin, Galen and Mia. They died exactly the way you said they did. That part of your story is true. But there was no third body, not in the woods where you said, not anywhere. There was no blood on any of your clothing, no cuts on your body from the devil's walkingstick. And there's no record of anyone named Rob Gear at your school, in your city. None of Mia's and Galen's friends have even heard the name. Just Liam."

"But . . . I killed Liam."

"By strangling him?" the doctor said.

"Yes! I've been totally honest with you from the start."

"You may have been honest with me, but you haven't been honest with yourself. Everything you told me that happened to you and Mia and Galen, I think that's mostly true. But everything that happened that was just between you and Liam? I think that's a lie. You stole the satellite phone, and you lit the fire in the barrel before the three of you headed off on that hike. You poked those holes in the gas tank, and you killed Galen, probably with the hammer after you followed him and Mia over to the Brummits' cabin. And later you put the rat poison in her cereal. As for whether Mia really ran over you on your bike, I don't know. But your medical records show you were in a bad bike accident, so I suspect that part's true too."

We stared at each other. I tried to laugh again, but this time my mouth wouldn't move. The tattoo on my wrist was still itching something fierce, so this time I scratched it, but it didn't help. Right away, it started itching again.

"There were four of us at the cabin," I insisted.

"No," the doctor said patiently. "Just three."

"This doesn't make any sense!"

"It actually makes a lot of sense. All those years around Mia and her friends, pretending to be someone you're not. It became like a second nature to you. But when you finally went through with what you were planning, when you killed Mia and Galen two weekends ago, you surprised yourself by feeling guilty afterward. It was one thing to *imagine* getting back at Mia, to plan and dream about it. The reality was something far different. But by then it was too late to change it. The past was the past, and Mia and Galen were dead. So you dealt with the guilt the way you'd dealt with a lot of things over the years—by compartmentalizing. By splitting your personality. You killed 'Liam,' then invented a new personality, 'Rob,' to keep yourself blameless. He was a victim of Liam's, along with

Mia and Galen. But unlike Mia and Galen, he was smart and resourceful enough to fight back, to defeat Liam. That's the story you tell yourself. Unfortunately, Rob's not real. His entire existence, every single thing you told me he did and thought, is a lie."

I didn't know what to say. What do you say when someone makes up a crazy whopper like that? I was one hundred percent sure it was a lie. But I still couldn't make myself laugh.

"I've told you all this before," the doctor said. "We've *done* all this before. You don't remember, but that's okay. I listen just the same. And I heard something in your story yesterday that I'd never noticed before. So today I listened for it again, and I heard it again. It's something that I think is a very good sign."

"What's really going on here?" I said. "What kind of joke is this? Are you trying to drive me crazy?"

"Listen to me, Liam," the doctor said. "This is very important. The story you told me? Never once did Rob and Liam speak to each other, not unless they were alone. And no one except Liam ever referred to Rob by name. You told me everything you were thinking at the time, but the way you spoke, the specific things you said, it could just as well have been Liam talking. It could have been Liam there alone."

"That's not . . ."

"Because it *was* Liam there alone. Do you understand?"

I thought about what the doctor was saying.

But then I shook my head. "It was a coincidence," I said. "Assuming that's the way I even did tell the story. Or are you one of those doctors who don't believe in coincidences?"

"I think it's the way you *always* tell the story."

"Then what does it mean?"

"It's a tell, Liam, like Mia said. It means your subconscious mind is trying to tell us that part of the story's a lie. Rob couldn't talk to Liam when others were there, because you *are* Liam. There's only one of you—there was *always* only one of you. And deep down, I think you know this. I think on some level, you want to rejoin the world of reality. That's why I think this is a very, very good sign."

My tattoo itched, even worse than before, but I didn't scratch it again. What was the point? Out of the corner of my eye, I saw a housefly skitter along the windowsill, but I didn't swat it either. I just knew what the doctor would have to say about my doing that.

"I want to leave," I said. "You can't keep me here against my will."

"Liam, listen to me," he said. "Before we can begin the next part of your treatment, you need to accept the truth. You need to accept that you're Liam Linard, and that you alone were responsible for all the horrible things that happened up at that cabin."

I didn't move a muscle. I thought about what the doctor was saying, thought about it for a very long time. Was there any chance, even the slightest percentage, he was telling the truth?

Finally, I turned to look at the fly on the windowsill. Now I saw it couldn't have been moving because it was dead on its back.

I looked back at the doctor.

"It was my fault," I said softly, but firmly. "Everything that happened that weekend."

He looked surprised, but pleased. "Really?"

I nodded sadly. "It's hard for me to admit that, but it's the truth. I was the one who suggested it in the first place. If I hadn't had the dumb idea to go away, who knows how things would've ended? Somehow, I'm going to have to live with that for the rest of my life."

Acknowledgments

Three people believed in this book long before anyone else: my husband, Michael Jensen; my agent, Jennifer De Chiara; and my editor, Michael Stother. They're the reason it exists in any form other than a file on my computer.

The folks at Simon & Schuster and Simon Pulse have also been extraordinarily supportive right from the beginning, especially Mara Anastas, Jon Anderson, Mary Marotta, Liesa Abrams, and my managing editor, Kayley Hoffman.

If a book is published and no one hears about it, was it still published? These folks have made sure that's not a question for this particular project: Lucille Rettino, Carolyn Swerdloff, Tara Greico, Anthony Parisi, Candace Greene McManus, Betsy Bloom, Michelle Leo, Christina Pecorale, Victor Iannone, Rio Cortez, and Danielle Esposito. And great book jackets don't design themselves—Steve Scott does.

Early readers who generously contributed their time and extremely helpful opinions include Liam Arne, Matt Browning, Matt Carrillo, Brian Centrone, Brian Dahlvig, Ulysses Dietz, Donna Gephart, Josh Loden, Peter Monn, Timothy Sandusky, and Peter Wright. David Lister and Scott Jarmon, thanks for the forensics tutorials, and Bill Middlebrook, thanks for showing me how to disable a car.

Finally, thanks as always to my assortment of creative genius friends: Tom Baer, Tim Cathersal, Lori Grant, Erik Hanberg, Marcy Rodenborn, James Venturini, and Sarah Warn.

About the Author

Brent Hartinger is the author of twelve novels. His first book, *Geography Club*, was adapted as a stage play and a feature film costarring Scott Bakula. Also a screenwriter, Brent has a number of other film projects under option and development.

In addition to his writing, Brent is the cohost of a podcast called Media Carnivores; a sometime member of the faculty at Vermont College in the MFA program in Writing for Children and Young Adults; and the founder of The Real Story Safe Sex Project, an HIV/AIDS education effort. In 1990, Brent also cofounded the world's third LGBT youth support group, in his hometown of Tacoma, Washington.

Brent now lives in Seattle with his husband, writer Michael Jensen. Read more by and about Brent, or contact him at brenthartinger.com.